H

THE

Howard Fast is well known for a literary career that spans more than sixty years. He is the author of over seventy novels, including *Spartacus, April Morning, Citizen Tom Paine, The Immigrants,* and *Freedom Road,* which has been published in eighty-two languages. Among most recent projects are the novels, *Redemption* and *An Independent Woman,* and the screenplay for *The Crossing,* a television movie for the A & E Television Network.

After the loss of his wife Bette—to whom this book was dedicated—he is now living happily in Connecticut with his new wife, Mercedes O'Connor.

COMING FROM ibooks

The Immigrants
by Howard Fast

AVAILABLE NOW

Are We Alone in the Cosmos?
The Search for Alien Contact in the New Millennium
Ben Bova and Byron Preiss, editors

Share your thoughts about these and other ibooks titles
in the new ibooks virtual reading group at
http://www.ibooksinc.com

THE
CROSSING

HOWARD FAST

ibooks
new york
www.ibooksinc.com

DISTRIBUTED BY SIMON & SCHUSTER, INC.

An Original Publication of ibooks, inc.

Pocket Books, a division of Simon & Schuster, Inc.
1230 Avenue of the Americas, New York, NY 10020

An ibooks, inc. Book

ibooks, inc.
24 West 25th Street
New York, NY 10010

The ibooks World Wide Web Site Address is:
http://www.ibooksinc.com

Share your thoughts about these and other ibooks titles
in the new ibooks virtual reading group at
www.ibooksinc.com

ISBN 0-671-03897-4
First Pocket Books printing November 1999
10 9 8 7 6 5 4 3 2 1

Cover design by Jason Vita
Cover photograph copyright © 1999 Andrew Eccles
Interior design by Michael Mendelsohn at MM Design 2000, Inc.

Printed in the U.S.A.

For my good friend, Paul R. Reynolds,
who gave me no peace until this book was written;
and for my wife, Bette,
whose love and patience made the writing possible.

List of Maps

Contents

Preface

The Crossing was my first attempt at American historiography; and though I had written several novels with the background of the American Revolution, I found that there was very little that expressed the truth of the Battle of Trenton. The formal historians characterized the battle as a murky miracle, and murky it was; nor did any one of the historians I read even mention that a flintlock musket, the Colonial weapon of the time, cannot be fired in the rain although that was the key to an understanding of the crossing.

Compared to the weapons of today, the flintlock was a primitive instrument. Powder had to be fed into the muzzle of the gun, and then a lead ball was jammed down the muzzle. Above the trigger was a powder pan with an opening into the barrel of the gun. A bit of gunpowder was dropped into this pan, and when the trigger was pulled, a flint would strike a metal tooth above the powder pan and ignite the gunpowder. This worked most of the time, but not all the time, and almost never in the rain. A phrase still in use, "a flash in the pan," describes the powder flashing in the firing pan without igniting the gun.

Knowing this, and realizing that when hostilities began, the Americans had no bayonets, or very few, and were armed for the most part with their hunting muskets, the British preferred—after their first two battles, Concord and Bunker Hill—to attack in rainy weather and to use the bayonet. Against the bayonets, the Americans had no defense.

In the battle for New York, they were slaughtered, both in Brooklyn and in Manhattan—which resulted in utter terror of a bayonet charge. Desperately, Washington called for bayonets, and by the time of the crossing, they had several thousand bayonets.

Finding the truth of that December night in 1776 was as exciting to my wife and myself as any detective story. We found old manuscripts that apparently had never been read during the 20th century. We traced and traveled the paths of the armies. We found letters written by Washington's staff officers, and finally we were able to put all the pieces of the puzzle together.

And indeed it was a puzzle, as you will see as you read what follows. At the time it was published, I took comfort that it was the first account of that December night in all of its detail.

For thirty years I have dreamed that some day this incredible story would be told in film—and at long last it has happened and *The Crossing* has become a film, produced by the Arts and Entertainment Network. I am grateful to them for their dedication to the project, and I hope that generations of Americans will profit from the retelling of the moment when the dream of a United States of America became a possibility.

Howard Fast
November 1999

Introduction

During filming of THE CROSSING I foolishly held out hope that I would become George Washington. Nothing schizophrenic, mind you, just a flicker where everything lined up and, in that elusive magical moment for which we actors train for years, it would happen, qualifying me to say with great authority to any talk show host who was willing to listen, "Yes, I felt him."

Well, sorry to say, it didn't happen. There was no bolt of lightning. No spirit in the night appeared. And once again, try as Hollywood might, I was left with the fact that no matter how hard an actor tries to frappé his instincts in with his exhaustive research, at the end of the day it's all make believe.

Still, the first time I read Howard's book, I was struck with the simplicity of his prose. He doesn't tell his story so much as present it and, in doing so, invokes the imagination to such a degree that before long, I'm there. He leaves it up to me to feel the cold. The exhaustion of marching for days without sleep. The fear of retreating from a force better equipped and better trained. The wearing away of their belief in what they were doing and why they were doing it and who was really this person leading them into one failure after another? Howard's words made me personalize it, as if leading me down the road, making me see and feel in as clear a way as possible that George Washington was not a myth, he was a man. And if you're an actor, that's all you need.

Howard's words begin in the middle of yet another Washington retreat, his troops deserting daily, his temper getting the better of him, barking commands almost irrationally. Outnumbered, outmaneuvered, and seemingly at odds with not only his enemy, but all those for whom he was fighting. As an actor, I constantly found myself stopping to envision Washington's state of mind at the crossroads of each predicament, the questions he asked of himself, the seemingly irresolvable situations with no possible exit and those times when he sat alone—always alone—thinking of yet another way out. Chapter after chapter, as the impossibility of the task increased, so did Washington's sense of responsibility to the cause. Howard's words were clear on one point: this country was founded by one man who kept his word. He alone stayed true to that which at one time was the will of so many. After all of the impassioned rhetoric and the intoxicating power of a rebellious 2nd Continental Congress, Washington was left to do it alone. He needed money. He needed supplies. He needed more men. His countless cries for assistance went unanswered until finally, with his troops sick and wounded and all but beaten, word came back from Congress that they were fleeing Philadelphia for Baltimore because they feared Washington "could not defend it."

Several weeks after we had finished shooting, I still found myself thinking about Washington. For reasons beyond me, America knows very little about him and his particular period in history. Sure, we know about the Monument in the nation's capital. Some of us have been to Mt. Rushmore. But we don't really know him, do we? I took a dollar bill out of my wallet and sat there staring at the face of the Father Of Our Country. I cannot honestly claim to have become him, but I can say with great authority that, after reading Howard's words and then having the opportunity to say and feel Howard's words, I can now see the man.

Jeff Daniels
August 6, 1999
St. Louis, MO

THE
CROSSING

THE
FIRST CROSSING

East to West

[1]

A T THE VERY BEGINNING, they did not think of themselves as soldiers. Most of them were deeply religious, with more of a feeling for life than for death. But in the twenty-four hours after the first meeting with the British regulars on Lexington Common, they got over their fear and they learned how to kill. Between the town of Concord in Massachusetts and Boston in Massachusetts, they tore a whole British army into shreds, sent it running back to Boston screaming in its pain; and it was then that their attitudes changed and they became cocky and contemptuous of every kind of British or European soldier.

From all over New England, from Vermont and New Hampshire and Maine and Massachusetts and Connecticut and Rhode Island, and from the midlands, New York, New Jersey and Pennsylvania, and even from Virginia and other places in the South, the people converged on Boston, where a British army was cornered with only a way out by sea. There were Minutemen and Committeemen and Militiamen

3

and musketeers and riflemen and pikemen off the fishing boats, youngsters, and grown men, all of them pouring into the Boston area, and at Bunker Hill they defeated the British again.

At Bunker Hill, they entrenched themselves and built earthworks, and the British marched full and flat against them, expecting them to panic and run away. But instead of fleeing, the Americans opened a deadly fire. The Americans gave way finally before the British, but they took a toll of almost a thousand of the enemy in dead and wounded.

And all this filled them with confidence and with contempt for their enemies, for men who "fight for hire."

A year later, having marched down from Boston to New York City, with a tall, skinny, long-nosed Virginian, George Washington, as their new commander in chief, they were more confident than ever. In all their lives and dreams they had never seen so many men together in one place as there were in New York on the ninth of July in 1776, when they were drawn up in their brigades to hear a public reading of the Declaration of Independence, written by a young man, Thomas Jefferson, and signed by the members of the Continental Congress. On that day, by actual count, there were 20,275 of them, tall, long-legged healthy lads, half of them under eighteen years old, and most of them cocky beyond belief.

The very number of them fed this feeling of security and superiority over the enemy, and every day additional groups of young volunteers, hot for freedom and full of pride, entered their camp. It was true that against them, Sir William Howe, the commander of the British army, could muster thirty thousand men—but his home base was over three thousand miles away, while theirs was just around the corner or across the river or over yonder a bit.

Anyway, if General Howe was foolish enough to attack them, they'd give him back his own coin in full measure. Most of the young men in the American army were farmers. Their fathers had let them go off after the planting but told them they were to get back for the harvest or get their necks wrung.

They could just look around at the army that was assembled here to know that it would all be over and done with long before harvest time.

[2]

THERE WERE FEW SECRETS in that curious war. There appears to have been a whole army of spies who would sell any bit of information to any buyer, and when Sir William Howe decided that he would land half of his army—fifteen thousand men—on the Brooklyn shore to take Long Island and perhaps cut off the Americans on Manhattan Island, the news soon got to Washington. He sat down to consult with his staff, among whom there was one officer, General Charles Lee, who was trained in the British army and of whom we will hear a good deal. Charles Lee was of the opinion that the British were stupid and rigid, and that they would go on repeating all the tactics that had led them to previous disaster. If the Americans made a show of force, the British would confront the rebels and attempt to brush them away.

Unfortunately, the great majority of General Washington's staff agreed with Lee. They were most of them bright, exuberant young men who felt that the one important problem was to get the British to fight, so that they might whip the daylights out of them.

The commander in chief was less young and exuberant than some of the others, but modest and unwilling to press his opinions or put himself forward as a military genius. He preferred to sit quietly in his beautiful buff-and-blue uniform, which had been tailored for his position as commander in the Virginia Militia and which was so admired that every officer who had the price had given orders to his own tailor to make him one of the same. After he had listened enough, it appeared to him that the counsel of these bright and articulate young officers made very good sense.

Thereupon, he worked out a scheme that might end the affair of the Revolution properly and quickly. He took eight thousand of his very best men, almost half of them riflemen and excellent marksmen, and had them ferried across the East River to Brooklyn. Their transportation across the river was contrived by a regiment of Massachusetts fishermen and sailors, who were under the command of Colonel John Glover; and once they were on the Brooklyn side, Washington had them take up positions on the high hill of Brooklyn Heights and there build earthwork barriers and trenches.

The reasoning behind this was very simple. The Americans would display indifference as to where the British landed on the Brooklyn shore. Actually, it did not matter where they landed, because wherever they came they would face the problem of the American position on Brooklyn Heights and the necessity to sweep it away before they could be secure in Brooklyn and ready to cut off the Americans in Manhattan. Thus, their landing would be unopposed. The British would step on shore, form their men in regiments and then march against the American position, and from behind their earthworks, the American riflemen would cut them down as they had at Bunker Hill.

However, Washington felt that there was a very real possibility that the landing in Brooklyn—so poorly kept secret—was no more than a diversion, and that the rest of the British forces would be directed against New York itself, perhaps in small boats from the great British ships of the line. Because it appeared so eminently sensible a course for his enemies to pursue, Washington kept the bulk of his artillery in New York, and his troops there on an even more intense alert than those in Brooklyn.

On August 22nd, fifteen thousand British and Hessian soldiers were landed at Gravesend Bay on the Brooklyn shore just south of the Narrows. Old Israel Putnam, a brave but rather simplistic soul, conceived of the astonishing notion of sending strong bodies of riflemen to take up positions in the woods facing the landing area. As the British advanced, the riflemen would shoot down the first ranks of the British and then retreat, leading the British army into the trap that awaited them on Brooklyn Heights.

And then the British refused to do any of the things that the Americans had planned for them. When the riflemen had taken up their positions in the woods, facing the main roads, the Hessians advanced on the double along little-used footpaths and cut off the riflemen, attacking them from the rear. Instead of wasting themselves in a frontal attack on the fortified positions on Brooklyn Heights, the British and Hessians concentrated on the slaughter and capture of the several thousand riflemen that had been sent out of the fortifications to intercept them.

Taken from behind, the riflemen—undisciplined at best—reacted in panic. They twisted around to fire at anything that moved and in many cases at their own comrades. Southerners and Pennsylvania woodsmen, their training was in the hunting of squirrel and deer, not men. Their long Pennsylvania rifles were difficult to load. The bullet had to be jammed down the long length of the barrel of the gun. And with those riflemen who preened themselves on an extra-long range and accurate weapon, the bullet actually had to be hammered into the barrel so that the inner screw literally threaded the soft lead.

Suddenly, their long, beautifully wrought rifles were worthless. In the fierce onslaught of the Hessian troops, there was not even time for the Americans to begin to load. If they turned to run away, the Hessians bayonetted them through the back. If they tried to club their long, unwieldly rifles and fight back, the Hessians drove in low and bayonetted them in the belly. In the thick woods, hand to hand, there was no more useless, more impossible weapon than the long Pennsylvania rifle.

The Americans threw down their guns and tried to surrender, but the Hessians would not let them. They and the British regiments had the smell of blood, and they killed until sheer exhaustion put an end to it. The screams of pain and terror from the dying Americans were so loud and awful that finally the blood-crazed English and Hessian officers came to their senses and stopped the slaughter and began the taking of prisoners.

But in the woods where the riflemen were trapped lay over six hundred American corpses unburied, unclaimed; how many exactly no one knows, for many of the riflemen were not on any official regimental roster, and for years afterward the place was known as the "wood of horror." Travelers spoke of the dreadful stink that emanated from the woods, and a whole mythology of ghostly terror tales arose concerning that bloody battlefield.

As far as the entrenchments on Brooklyn Heights were concerned, there too the British refused to behave as the Americans had decided that they would. Instead of launching a frontal attack upon the Americans, they began to unload the big guns from the ships of the line, so that they might blow the American position to pieces.

General Washington did not wait for this to happen. Shattered by the defeat, hundreds of his men and officers dead, hundreds more wounded and a great part of his Brooklyn army in the hands of the British as prisoners of war, he immediately ordered Colonel Glover to bring the men back to Manhattan. A strong wind from the north kept the British warships out of the East River, and if the military exercise in Brooklyn was wanting, the retreat was masterly. It was the first retreat from a lost battlefield by a man who would soon be known sardonically as the great master of military retreat.

[3]

THE COCKINESS PASSED, and a new mood, fear, pervaded the Americans. There were eyewitness stories, some of them invented and some of them real, and they were of three types. In one, the Hessian skewered the Yankee to a tree, and there he hung like a bug pinned on a board, the bayonet through his chest, screaming while he died. In the second, the Hessian stuck the Yankee lad through the genitals and drove the bayonet up into his guts, and in the third story, the Hessian stabbed the fleeing Yankee in the back. All three were sufficiently terrifying. A German regiment of farmboys from Bucks County, Pennsylvania, had taken to calling the Hessians *"Die Jäger der Hölle"* (the foresters from hell), even though there was only one Jäger regiment among the many Hessian regiments that fought the Americans in Brooklyn. The Hessians were as good as any soldiers in Europe. But now they were magnified out of all proportion to reality and turned into objects of consuming terror.

A crack Rhode Island rifle regiment of two hundred men disappeared one night, and then during the following few days, over four thousand Massachusetts and Connecticut men deserted and disappeared from the camp. It was a panic so uncontrollable that for a few days, General Washington came to believe that his army was beyond hope or redemption. A whole regiment of riflemen from South Carolina, who had grumbled incessantly that the war would be over before they saw an Englishman in the sights of their rifles, picked up and marched out of camp, north to a ferry across the Hudson and then back home. Even the threat of cannon facing them did not stop them, and young Henry Knox, in command of the artillery, lacked the stomach to give an order for Americans to fire on Americans.

The plain truth was that the morale of the riflemen had been shattered. It was almost impossible to fix a bayonet onto the end of one of the long, slender Pennsylvania rifles—certainly beyond the skill of the metalworkers available in New York—and without a bayonet, these soldiers lacked the will to face the enemy. Washington had looked upon his thousands of riflemen as a sort of secret weapon, superb marksmen who would cut down the red-coats before the attacking British could ever approach to bayonet distance. But the reality had proved quite different. The tall, swaggering, buckskin-clad bullies, with their fringed shirts and their carved powderhorns, were beyond training. They drank too much, quarreled incessantly and looked upon any sort of discipline as a direct threat to their honor, as they put it. Loudmouthed, foul-tongued as many of them were, they posed a constant threat to the entire structure of the new army. After the slaughter on Brooklyn Heights, they boasted no longer. Within two weeks, half of the riflemen had deserted, fleeing the camp by night for the most part—nor were they ever again to be a decisive factor in the American Revolution, although some regiments, the Bennington Rifles of Vermont and a number of Pennsylvania and Virginia regiments, performed bravely throughout the war.

[4]

IN THE COLD, bitter reality of defeat and death, an army was born, and this is the story of their borning and of the agony that went with it—and how awful in those birth pangs was the realization of what war is and what happens to men who fight. Most of the army was very young, but in the weeks that followed the 22nd of August in 1776, their youth passed away. They became old with the aging that only the intimate knowledge of death brings. They learned that when a soldier retreats before an invader in his own land, he leaves a little bit of himself behind every step of the way. His retreat is thus limited and conditioned by death, and it has a point of no return.

In our story, this point was the Delaware River, the natural boundary between the two rich colonies of New Jersey and Pennsylvania, and it is this river that is specific in the crossing; and ours is the story of how the skinny fox hunter from Virginia and his frightened men crossed it twice.

[5]

A WORD MUST BE SAID here about the table of organization of this Army of the Revolution led by Washington. Beginning at the bottom, there were the companies, and they were put together in a dozen different ways. Many of them were of Minutemen or Committeemen, who had been drilling on their village greens for months before the hostilities started. The drilling was fun and socially pleasant, but it did not make them into soldiers. Others were religious companies: Methodists or Presbyterians or Baptists. There were fewer of these. Then there were the lodges, Masonic companies, fellowship companies, trade companies such as fuller and cooper and ropewalker and bookbinder and many others, and then the class companies of rich men and their youngsters in beautiful tailored uniforms and, of course, there were the regular militia companies for defense against the red men and bandits and outlaws.

A number of companies, geographically connected, as in town or county or colony, were logged together as regiments. Most of the companies were commanded by captains, who were usually assisted by one or two or five lieutenants. The number of lieutenants depended upon the size of the company—from forty to a hundred men at the beginning—and also upon how many young officers could

afford saddle horses and tailored uniforms. The regiment—
and all of this applies only to the first months of the war—
would consist of from two to ten companies. It was
commanded by a colonel, a man whose command derived
from prior military experience, or from his wealth, or from
his position in the community or from his education, for
these were a people dedicated to education and deeply
impressed by it.

Two or five or ten regiments—again depending upon
size—would be logged together as a brigade, and this would
be under the command of a brigadier or brigadier general.
These general officers who commanded the brigades of
General Washington's army were as unusual a group of
men as this continent ever saw associated in a single
effort—doctors, lawyers, merchants, college professors,
teachers, professional soldiers who had left the British army
to fight with the Americans, planters, builders, saintly men,
drunkards, scoundrels, cheats, liars—but in their great
majority men of high purpose and integrity. In other words,
they were precisely the kind of collection of men such a situation as the American Revolution would produce.

Over the brigadiers was the commander in chief, who
was directly responsible to the Congress of the Colonies.

[6]

HE ALSO FEET RESPONSIBLE to his brigadiers. A week
after the defeat in Brooklyn, he called them together to talk
about whether they should try to defend New York City and
Manhattan Island against the British fleet and army or
whether they should retreat and take up their position in a
better place. As always, his general staff was divided; and

as was often the case, the division was between those who had been trained in foreign military establishments and those who were volunteer soldiers out of American civilian life. The professionals looked down upon the Americans, both as soldiers and as colonials.

General Roche de Fermoy led the trend of professional opinion in the belief that New York City could be held. This was boastful and impractical, but Fermoy still commanded a Pennsylvania rifle regiment that had been untouched by Brooklyn Heights. He insisted that the British soldiers could be picked off if they were to leave their great warships and attempt a landing. There was considerable sourness about riflemen in battle, and such civilian general officers as Nathanael Greene and William Alexander had the deepest respect for the huge ships of the line that had anchored in the Upper Bay and in the Hudson River. Like Washington, they were involved in a venture upon which they had staked life and family, and they were desperately eager not to be caught in a trap.

The result of the argument among the general officers was that the commander in chief allowed himself to be pressed into a ridiculous compromise, and against all his better judgment. In time, he would trust only himself because there was no alternative. But now he was still the amiable amateur, trying to please everyone. And even though he had told those closest to him that he believed the city could not be held, and even though he knew the danger of risking his cause on an island when the British controlled the water, he allowed himself to be talked into dividing his army. Five thousand men were retained for the defense of New York City and Manhattan Island, and nine thousand were sent to build a fortified position at the little village of Kingsbridge in the Bronx. Two thousand more were stationed in the northern part of Manhattan.

Sixteen thousand in all. Eight days before, he had commanded over twenty thousand men. The attrition was terrifying, and he and his officers knew that it had only begun.

Another week, and the British made their second move. They sailed their great warships into Kip's Bay, and began a thunderous cannonade of the beach, while the British regulars and marines were carried ashore by landing boats. Anticipating the move by watching the progress of the ships, Washington had stationed riflemen on the shore to pick off the British soldiers in the landing boats. But when the cannonading began, the riflemen panicked. It was simply too close to the memories of Brooklyn Heights, and the riflemen threw down their guns and ran away. Washington and Nathanael Greene charged down on the fleeing men, screaming and swearing and threatening them—and eventually they caused some line of battle to be formed. But it was too late. New York City was lost.

The American army fled on the double, and Washington organized them into a line of defense across the whole of Manhattan Island about seven miles to the north, just beyond the deep valley of Harlem, which was then called the Hollow Way.

Entrenched on Harlem Heights above the Hollow Way, Washington and his generals took heart. This was the strongest position they had held since the Battle of Bunker Hill, and since they commanded every road north through Manhattan, the British would have to march against them and sweep them out of the way.

But General Howe was past the stage of marching against hilltops where the Americans crouched in ditches. After a brief testing of the defenses, he embarked his army in the warships and sailed up the Sound to Westchester. Now he was behind the Americans, and their defense of Manhattan Island became meaningless.

The Americans had built a strong fort on the high ridge of northern Manhattan, facing the Hudson River, and they had named it Fort Washington, in honor of their commander in chief. The Americans now moved there, while Washington himself rode into Westchester to meet the British landing party. At the Battle of White Plains, in October, the Continental troops once again failed to halt the British advance.

Washington crossed over to New Jersey, hoping they could hold Fort Washington in Manhattan. But again, the British refused to march head on into an American trap, and they brought up to Fort Washington a great concentration of heavy cannon. Then, for hours, they poured artillery fire into the earthworks until they were leveled. When the cannon smoke cleared, the American defenders saw a column of Scottish Highlanders, advancing behind their skirling pipes with bayonets fixed, and on either side of them, the dreaded Hessians. The Hessians were led by Colonel Rahl, a fearless officer whom we will meet again. He was recognized, and his name added to the general terror.

In a sense, Fort Washington collapsed under its own pervading fear. The Americans holding the outer earthworks expected an attack on the fairly level landward side. But Colonel Rahl had led his Hessians up the steep, brush-covered rocks that dropped down to the Hudson River on the west side of the fort. When they appeared at the earthworks with naked bayonets, the Americans abandoned their positions and fled to the main redoubt for protection. Suddenly, the central redoubt was a mass of panic-stricken soldiers who had neither the wit nor the desire to turn and face the enemy and fight.

Hundreds of other Americans broke out of the fort, leaped past the earthworks and tumbled head over heels down the rocky slope to the Hudson. Some managed to cross the river and join the American army on the other side, but those were only a handful. Most of those who escaped hid in the thickets on the Manhattan shore, north to the Isham Heights, where a great and magnificent forest of tulip trees surrounded an old Indian village, a shelter as lonely and untouched as one could find. They hid in this forest and subsequently made their way north and homeward, deserting, as so many others were doing.

But by far the majority of the garrison of Fort Washington were taken captive, over two thousand unwounded men in all. A dozen others were injured. And while tremendous tales were contrived later concerning the gallantry of the men who defended the fort, the bitter truth is that it was given away, with only twelve men killed among the defenders.

Across the Hudson River, on the Palisades, General Washington and his brigadiers watched as the enemy flag was raised through the clouds of smoke that lay over the fort. What thoughts crossed his mind then, we will never know. But certainly he must have reflected ruefully that the first place ever named in his honor had made a speedy transition. Possibly, he also felt that it might well be the last. And he might have thought to himself that it was high time he stopped taking the advice of others, for he wrote to his brother Augustine:

"This is a most unfortunate affair, and has given me great mortification; as we have lost not only two thousand men that were there, but a good deal of artillery and some of the best arms we had. And what adds to my mortification is that this post, after the last ships went past it, was held contrary to my wishes and opinion . . ."

Such was the chaos of the moment that Washington actually did not have the full figure of the loss. Sir William Howe, the British commander, ordered a count, and the total was 2,818 men and officers. By midnight, the count was finished, and the poor, damned men were marched off under guard to New York City, there to rot and die in the British prison ships.

[7]

THERE HE WAS, fox hunter and aristocrat and not too bad with cards and women; but he had nothing to boast about as a soldier or a leader of soldiers. He had ordered his own count on the Fourth of July, that hot, sunny, lovely day when 20,275 of his men paraded on the green in New York City. Now, on the twentieth of November, he took another count not by head, for his army was in three places, part of it at North Castle on the Hudson under the command of General Lee, part of it at Fort Lee, which was on the Palisades, across the Hudson River from Fort Washington and part of it with him at Hackensack a few miles from Fort Lee. So it was a count not by head but by addition, putting together what he hoped was left to him. The putting-together amounted to no more than eleven thousand men—and even that was dwindling away as he totaled his figures. Five months and ten thousand men gone.

But at least let them be together. This was his main thought, as he wrote to General Lee: ". . . the public interest requires your coming over to this side of the Hudson with the Continental troops . . .", writing respectfully, for General Lee was no dunderhead like himself but a professional military man, and he had not lost an army twice, as had a fox hunter from Virginia. In fact, General Lee was the darling of thousands of Americans, which goes to explain why they named the fort on the Palisades after him.

But Lee ignored the letter, and then a message came from General Greene, who was in command at Fort Lee. The British warships had sailed up the Hudson, and now they were disembarking an army, thousands of men and guns and wagons of supply on the shore about six miles above Fort Lee. It was too late to stop them, for they already held the shoreline and the heights above it.

Washington called for his horse, mounted and rode like the very devil for the fort. He rode so hard that Alexander Hamilton, his young aide who was under twenty, was put to it to keep up with him.

But there was no sprig of hope at Fort Lee. Greene told Washington that scouts found that the British army was marching inland into Jersey, so as to cut off the Americans, pin them onto the Palisades, and make an end of them once and for all.

"Then what in God's name are we waiting for?" Washington demanded.

Greene tried to explain. They had lost guns and sup-

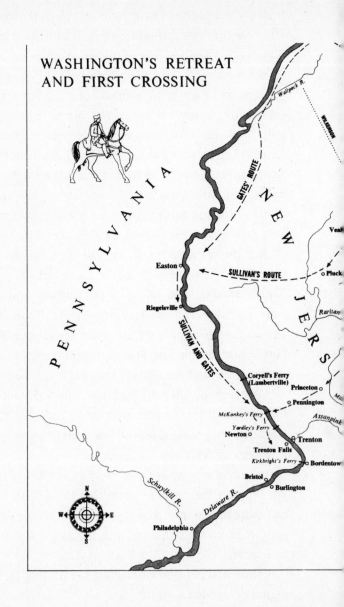

WASHINGTON'S RETREAT
AND FIRST CROSSING

Wallpack R.

WALLPACK

GATES' ROUTE

N E W

Veal

Easton

SULLIVAN'S ROUTE

Pluck

Riegelsville

Raritan

J E R S

SULLIVAN AND GATES

P E N N S Y L V A N I A

Coryell's Ferry
(Lambertville)

Princeton

Pennington

Mill

McKonkey's Ferry

Assanpink

Yardley's Ferry
Newton

Trenton

Trenton Falls

Kirkbright's Ferry

Bordentow

Bristol

Schuylkill R.

Delaware R.

Burlington

N

W   E

S

Philadelphia

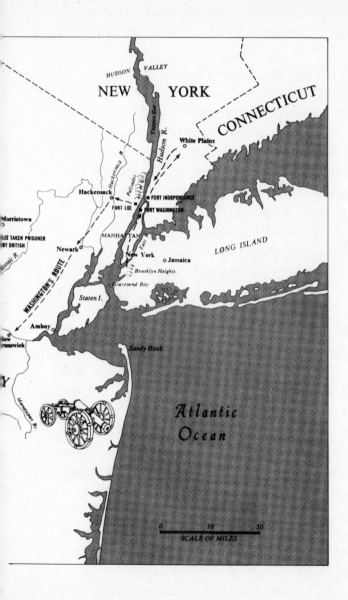

HUDSON VALLEY

NEW YORK

CONNECTICUT

Tappan Zee

Hudson R.

White Plains

Hackensack R.

Palisades

Hackensack

Morristown

■ FORT INDEPENDENCE

FORT LEE ■ ■ FORT WASHINGTON

LEE TAKEN PRISONER
BY BRITISH

Passaic R.

Newark

MANHATTAN

New York ○ Jamaica

WASHINGTON'S ROUTE

Brooklyn Heights

Gravesend Bay

LONG ISLAND

Staten I.

Amboy

New Brunswick

Y

Sandy Hook

Navesink R.

Atlantic
Ocean

0   10   20
SCALE OF MILES

plies in Brooklyn, and more at Kip's Bay and still more at Fort Washington. Now it would take at least four or five hours to load their supplies and to find horses to pull the guns.

Within five minutes, the army was leaving Fort Lee. Let all be lost, all but the men. A naked man could be clothed and armed, but where was the gun that would find a man? Washington had come to realize the value of men, and he treasured them like some miser who had lost half his fortune. When the men marched, it was not enough for him, and he drew his sword and whipped them on with the flat of it. "Run! Run!" he shouted.

"Run! Run!" his aides shouted.

"Run!" the other officers shouted.

"Run!" was the scream that went out.

"Faster!"

"Faster!" he yelled, bearing down on them with his big white horse, and many was the man who nursed the welts from the flaying sword of the Virginian.

The cooking kettles were abandoned with soup and meat bubbling smartly. The big iron guns, the tents and blankets and ammunition and stores of food, all were left to the enemy. And thousands of men were running headlong down that steep little dirt road that swept from Fort Lee to the meadows and across the meadows, past all the prissy little Dutch houses to the wooden bridge that spanned the Hackensack River.

Before all crossed the bridge, the British came into sight, hooting and deriding the dirty Continentals who knew nothing else but to run away.

There were a few cannon left in the encampment at

Hackensack, and Hamilton had dashed out in front of the fleeing army and reached the encampment, where he and Henry Knox loaded a cannon with grapeshot and dragged it to cover the bridge. When the last fleeing American was across, Knox and Hamilton stood over their primed cannon with a flaming match, both of them weeping with vexation.

But the British remained beyond cannon shot and had a good laugh. The Scottish Highlanders strutted in their natty kilts, and the pipers swaggered back and forth, keeping the pipes skirling until late into the night.

[8]

CHARLES CORNWALLIS, who led the British army in New Jersey, was told by Sir William Howe to make a quick end of Washington, his army and the war. Lord Cornwallis had a reputation for ferocity that was perhaps deserved and a reputation for military intelligence that was unmerited. It was not that the British were unable to learn—albeit they learned slowly—but that having once absorbed the lesson, it took them so long to unlearn. Having discovered during the Battle of Concord that one did not march between stone walls that might shelter Continentals, they scouted every stone wall on a Jersey roadside before marching through. Having learned during the Battle of Bunker Hill that it did not pay to advance uphill against a position the Continentals held, they put a thin skirmish line over every hill before they mounted it. They never entered a wood without beating through it first, and they avoided swampy areas where they might have been entrapped.

Thus Washington and his army were saved for the

moment. It was not that Cornwallis was afraid of the Americans; quite to the contrary, he had the utmost contempt for them and saw no reason to lose a single man to this rag-tail, dying army. He was content to march after them, waiting for the moment when he could bring the frightened rabble to bay on a proper battlefield, and then destroy them.

Washington, on the other hand, desired only to survive. Each day that he awakened with an army still in existence was a particular triumph, and for the moment he asked no more. Desertions were going on at the rate of about one hundred men a day, and he saw no way to halt them, short of turning the guns upon his own men. This he would not do—although some of his general officers advised it—and it is likely that if he had attempted to halt desertions by musket balls, his entire army would have disintegrated.

Turning and twisting, destroying every bridge he crossed, Washington covered over a hundred miles between Fort Lee and the Delaware River just north of Trenton, and early on Saturday, December 7, 1776, he reined his big white horse down the steep slope to the banks of the river. The road was muddy and treacherous, for it had rained on and off for days, and in good part the wretched weather accounted for the fact that they had come safely through the past seventeen days of retreat. The British could not move faster than their great supply wagons, their big artillery pieces—some of them shipboard thirties mounted on giant carriages—and their heavily loaded caissons. Again and again, the iron-wheeled vehicles were mired in the mud, holding up the entire army. On one day, driving his men to their limit, Cornwallis managed to cover twenty miles, but this exhausted the army so that it hardly moved the following day, waiting hours for all the stragglers to appear; and generally speaking, their progress was no more than ten miles a day. This, together with the need to rebuild bridges before rivers could be crossed, saved Washington. And even if it had crossed Cornwallis's mind to break loose from his guns and baggage and simply sweep down on Washington with musket and bayonet alone, he knew that such a radical departure from British military technique might well destroy him—for if he failed, no plea in his own behalf would be accepted.

Tom Paine was with the army during this retreat from Fort Lee. He was a sort of civilian-soldier—for the line between the two was very uncertain then—and though he carried a musket, he was not attached to any brigade, but existed rather in the way of a war correspondent, perhaps the first of the line. His *Common Sense* was the most widely read book in the colonies, and his name was known everywhere. Washington liked him, and they spent hours together discussing the war and what hope and meaning—if any—might be extracted from it then.

Afterward, in his first *Crisis* paper, Paine wrote:

"With a handful of men, we sustained an orderly retreat for near a hundred miles, brought off our ammunition, all our field pieces, the greatest part of our stores, and had four rivers to cross. None could say that our retreat was precipitate, for we were three weeks in performing it that the country might have time to come in. Twice we marched back to meet the enemy and remained out until dark. The sign of fear was not seen in our camp; and had not some of the cowardly and disaffected inhabitants spread false alarms through the country the Jerseys had never been ravaged."

In his enthusiasm, Paine was a little less than forthright.

They had not brought their stores from Fort Lee, but had left everything to the enemy. They had retreated for seventeen days, not three weeks, and at times their retreat had been utterly precipitate. But Paine's purpose was to recruit, not to further disintegration.

[9]

IT WAS WASHINGTON HIMSELF who held onto the reality, who remained calm and was thoughtful and gentle from day to day. In his own quiet way, he noticed and remembered things, and used them when they had to be used. Casting about desperately for some way out of their predicament, some path to survival, he remembered the Durham boats and began to build a concept around them. This time, he asked for no one's counsel, but proceeded on his own.

It makes sense that Washington would know about the Durham boats, monster freight carriers, some of them as much as sixty feet in length, eight feet in the beam and three and a half feet in the depth of hold. They were shallow-water boats, loading fifteen tons of dead weight and still drawing no more than thirty inches of water. Because he knew about them, something of the world was changed.

He met and talked with John Glover. There was no way he could reach Glover and very likely there was no way Glover could reach him. When they sat in the commander in chief's tent during that wretched retreat, with the pouring rain beating at the canvas outside and falling from it in tiny droplets from the inside, they were no closer than before. Long-nosed, tight-lipped, Presbyterian by religion, New Englander by birth, fisherman by trade, merchant by instinct, tightfisted, hard-nosed, John Glover bristled at the very sight of the tall, gentle-spoken Potomac aristocrat. That they should be on the same side in the same army was miracle enough; John Glover of Marblehead, Massachusetts, could find no reason under God for liking the Virginian.

Perceptive people like John Adams suggested that John Glover had saved the Virginian's life and honor once too often for any love to exist between them. In a way it was true. After the debacle at Brooklyn, it was John Glover and his Massachusetts fishermen who plucked the remnants of the American army from the Brooklyn shore and bore them back to Manhattan. Up in Westchester, the only forces that opposed Sir William Howe's landing were the same fishermen, and the same men, Glover leading them, took Washington and his army across the Tappan Zee into Jersey, and then the few survivors of Fort Washington out from under the noses of the British and across the Hudson River. Always, it was John Glover and his sailors and his fishermen—always when the "lousy, Papist" Southerners had dropped the whole mess into hot water.

So it is not hard to imagine the conversation between the two of them, there in that tent:

"I intend to cross the Delaware and hold the shore. I intend to run no more."

"Oh?" And then John Glover must have asked just how the general proposed to cross a river swollen like the very devil under this constant rain, and where would they find the boats? And even if there were a few rotten little scows, you don't put an army across a river in rowboats, and did he know how long it would take to put this army across in the few boats they might find?

"How long?"

"A week."

"The British are ten miles away. We must cross the river in a matter of hours after we reach the bank."

John Glover's temper hung on a thin thread. He would remind the Virginian that everyone else deserted. Even this general had desertions in his own precious lifeguards, but the fishermen stayed. But because they stayed you didn't expect miracles from them.

Then it would have taken the same path of all the other meetings with Glover. Washington would have flattered and cozened him, and finally, the Virginian would have spoken about the Durham boats.

Glover might not have known about the Durham boats or ever seen one of them, because he was a New England man, and the Durham boats were used to freight iron down from Riegelsville, where it was smelted and cast at the Durham furnace. There was a whole fleet of the great Durham boats making the run between Riegelsville and Philadelphia, and Washington could not have spent the time he did in Philadelphia without seeing the big ore boats tied up at the wharves.

He would have described the boats to Glover, and Glover's eyes would have lit up at talk of—according to Knox—the only thing he loved or cared for, a ship or a gig or a boat. And he might have said:

"If these Durham boats are what you say they are, and if you can gather together twenty of them, and if we can put thirty men or a pair of nags or a load of cannon into one of them, then I'll take your army across the damn river, I will."

HE HAD STATED ONCE—in his own curious manner—that
his honor forbade him to have secrets from the Congress,
and on December I, from his camp at New Brunswick, listening to the pouring rain, he wrote to Congress as follows:

"I have sent forward Colonel Hampton to collect proper
boats and craft at the ferry for transporting our troops, and
it will be of infinite importance to have every other craft,
besides what he takes for the above purpose, secured on the
west side of the Delaware, otherwise they may fall into the
enemy's hands and facilitate their views."

His language to Congress was always formal, polite, and
very often separated by an enormous barrier of manners
from the reality of his situation. To "facilitate" the "views"
of the enemy meant to permit the enemy to destroy him.
His writing reflected nothing of the enormous change that
had come about inside of him. He called into his tent two
very hard-minded and dependable Virginia gentlemen
whom he had known in the old times, Wade Hampton and
General William Maxwell. Maxwell was a tough Irishman
who had left the poverty and servitude of Ireland behind
him to find meaning and purpose in America and his own
soul in the Revolution. He was one of Washington's close
circle of personal friends, whom he leaned on and depended on. He asked them whether they knew what the Durham
boats were.

They had seen them.

He then told him that he wanted those Durham boats.

"Do we pay for them?"

With what, he might have asked them. For months now,

he and his friends had been paying out of their own pock-ets—when they had the money—for everything from food to information. Congress had no money. No, they were not to pay for the Durham boats. They were to take them.

And the iron works?

To hell with the iron works! he might have said, but even more richly, for there was no one who served under him who did not attest to his fine command of language. They were to take the boats. Oh, they could give paper for them, receipts, or kill anyone who tried to stop them or do whatever they damn well had to do, but they were to go with mounted men, and in three days he wanted those boats at McKonkey's Ferry landing on the Jersey shore of the Delaware River.

In three days? Didn't he understand that it was impos-sible in three days or six or ten?

He understood nothing of the kind; and furthermore, he told them, they were to destroy every other boat on the river, up the river thirty miles, down the river thirty miles—every boat on the Jersey shore was to be smashed to smithereens, beyond repair. Burn them, warm yourselves on the damn boats. Washington wanted only the Durham boats on the river.

Suppose the people were to take their boats over to Pennsylvania?

If they could trust them.

So something had happened to the man who led them, and he was different.

He told them to take a hundred men on horseback.

Do we have a hundred horses?

They would damn well find a hundred mounted men, or he'd know the reason why. They were to take the men on horses and keep on moving, and the commander in chief could not care less whether they slept and whether they ate, but they were to keep on moving and get the boats. That was all he cared about at this moment—the Durham boats.

Without the Durham boats it was all over.

[11]

MEN WHO PERFORM SMALL MIRACLES are frequently too occupied to note the circumstances properly. Hampton and Maxwell got the Durham boats, at least twenty of them and possibly as many as thirty; we are not sure of the precise number. They didn't do it in three days, but by the fifth of December, the first boats were steered into the ferry land-ing, where Colonel Glover and his men were putting together a crude embarkation dock. An hour after daylight on the seventh of December, the vanguard ranks of the beaten, shivering Continental army came into sight, and they were hustled into the big Durham boats by the New England fisherman. Whatever John Glover put his hand to, he did well, and this crossing was no exception.

The first boat pushed off, thirty men as passengers and a dozen fishermen at the poles and sweeps; and the next boat began to load. It was Saturday, but Reverend McWhorter, a Presbyterian minister from Newark who had attached himself to the army as a sort of general chaplain, hastened the Sabbath and put up his folding lectern and prepared for services. The rain had stopped, and it was a sunny, glorious winter morning. Since there was nothing much else to do while waiting for their turn to cross over, the Reverend found himself with the largest congregation of his career and with the satisfaction of knowing that a considerable number of Methodists and Baptists were included in his audience, as well as a sprinkling of Papists, Jews, Quakers and Free-thinkers. He preached the sins of the British, and if there was a good deal of talking and hooting in his congregation, there was also considerable amazement. It was said afterward that this was the first time on the American continent that a Presbyterian minister preached without noting sinfulness in his own congregation—although in the back rows, there were over two hundred bedraggled women, camp followers most of them, who had stuck with the army through better and worse, mostly worse.

By late afternoon of the following day, the army was across the river and safe—at least for the moment—in Bucks County, Pennsylvania. The New England fishermen and their leader, John Glover, had taken them across in the huge Durham boats as nicely—as one of them put it—as any load of codfish. It is said that even as the last boat was pushing off, the skirling of Lord Cornwallis's pipers was heard in the distance, those whom the Reverend McWhorter called "Papist Highland barbarians," ignoring the fact that most of them were of his own faith. And it is also said that the Americans fired their muskets and gave the colonial equivalent of a Bronx cheer to the kilted Highlanders. But it is more probable that the entire army was safely across before Cornwallis reached the river bank, even though Cornwallis had marched his men on the double for five hours once he finally realized that the "old fox," as they had begun to call the stubborn Virginian, had dug up something larger than river skiffs.

Too slow and too late, though Cornwallis understood it

not at all. If he had come on five hours earlier, he could have pinned Washington and the dying army to the Jersey bank, and there, the river behind them, the fierce High-landers and Hessians in front of them, the war might have been over.

But from Cornwallis's point of view, it was already finished. The sight of the Continental army in full flight down the road from Fort Lee to Hackensack would linger long with the British officers, and one might think of them, sitting their horses on the bank of the Delaware River in the early winter sunset and saying, good riddance to bad rubbish, for no army was left, no threat and surely no hope for the rebel cause.

And they might have said all this with reason, for safe across the river, able to breathe deeply and slowly for the first time in four months of defeat and flight, General Washington took stock of what he had rescued out of disaster:

Four months ago, he had had twenty thousand men—and better, all of them healthy enough to march and fight.

Now he had somewhat over six thousand men by count. But of the six thousand, almost seven hundred were unable to walk, so sick from disease and wounds that they had to ride in carts or be carried by their comrades; and a thousand more were ambulatory ill, differing from the stretcher cases only in that they could still drag their sick bodies with no more help than a crutch or a comrade's arm.

A hundred miles to the north of him, about a thousand of his men were under the leadership of General Horatio Gates. Washington had left Gates with seven depleted regiments to guard the Hudson River Valley for a while. But then when he needed those men, Gates ignored him, pretended not to receive his messages and would not come to him. And somewhere in western New Jersey was another part of his army, some two thousand men under the leadership of General Charles Lee. And Lee too had disappeared with his army and ignored messages, and might well have been destroyed for all that Washington knew. Both these sections were under the leadership of professional British officers, who had deserted the British for whatever gain or riches or fame might lie with the American cause.

But Washington had no real hope on December 7 that these two bodies of men could elude the British forces on the Jersey side of the Delaware River. He had no other hope than the ragged, beaten army he still led.

[12]

BUT WHEN WASHINGTON AWAKENED, the following morning, after a few hours of sleep, it was to the friendly sound of church bells tolling in a place where his shattered army would be sheltered and protected. New York and New Jersey had been a jungle, both colonies torn by inner strife and often by what amounted to civil war. There were whole counties in New York and New Jersey that belonged to the Tories, where rebel families had been rooted and driven out, tarred and feathered and sometimes shot or hanged. Bands of Tories conducted their own warfare with bands of rebels, and every fence or tree could hold a friend or an enemy or highwaymen and bandits who were both.

Unlike New England, both Jersey and New York had been in large measure parceled out by the Crown in big estates, great manors of many thousands of acres. Bucks County in Pennsylvania was something else entirely. Originally explored by the Dutch, who only established a few trading posts, it was first settled by Swedes, who built log houses and laid down the log-cabin pattern for part of early America. Then the Dutch returned and took the land by right of conquest. But there was no friction between them and the Swedes, and they both prospered in the fertile valleys. In 1681 a grant was made to William Penn, and two years later he built his magnificent country residence at Pennsbury Manor near Tullytown. A diverse and interesting population of Swedes, Dutch, German immigrant farmers, English Quakers and suburbanites from Philadelphia settled in Bucks County.

In 1727, the Durham Mine Furnace was established, mining the ore they smelted from Rattlesnake Hill and from Iron Hill—and then Welsh charcoal burners moved into the neighborhood to provide fuel for the smelting—and in the first years of the furnace, Robert Durham designed and built the first Durham boat.

Not only was Bucks County well settled, well civilized and liberal in thought and action, but for the first time in months, Washington could feel that he was among his own people. All around him were the homes of cultured and friendly inhabitants, who were not only loyal to the cause he espoused but who had played major roles in bringing it into being.

It made a difference. The day before, he had been hounded like a hare before the pack; now, at noon, he sat at lunch with four of his general officers at the home of Thomas Barclay at Trenton Falls and once again, like a civilized man, found himself eating hot, risen bread and commenting on the quality of the Madeira wine, which Barclay knew he was fond of and had managed to get in anticipation of his coming.

A commander in chief needs a headquarters, even when his army is dying and his cause is perishing; and Thomas Barclay begged him to make it here, at his home. It was a big, commodious house, spacious enough for Washington and his servants, and Barclay was a man of substance, a merchant, and only too eager to go into his own pocket for the needs of these men who had come across the Delaware. Jersey and New York might be lost, but it was impossible for Barclay and his neighbors to believe that Pennsylvania, with its great, prosperous center of Philadelphia, could be given up. Six thousand men were still quite a number, and all one had to do was to look out of one of the windows in the Barclay house to see them milling about, gathering firewood, building fires, leading horses to and fro, and—where they could enlist the help of others in barbering—shaving.

It was a clean-shaven time, but here was a whole army with whiskers, a wonderful, amazing array of whiskers that no one had the time to crop, and along with the whiskers, long hair. It was well enough for the rich to cut their hair close and have a wig stand of a dozen pieces; a plain man used his own hair and kept it shoulder length in the ordinary course of things. But now, especially among the youngsters, the hair was waistlong, yellow and red and brown and black, and many of them, just to keep the hair in place, had taken to wearing it in one or two fat braids.

Hearing the reports over the past months, the people

of Bucks County, like the people in so many other parts of the colonies, might well have surrendered the cause to defeat. Yet here was the army, battered, shrunk—yet in being.

[13]

DURING THOSE FIRST FEW DAYS after the crossing, the army was stunned. Their lives had been fixed in a pattern of retreat and defeat; then what now—except to count the days? Of those who remained, seventy-five percent were enlisted for one year, 1776. It was the eighth, the ninth, the tenth of December; three weeks and the year would be over, and then, without ever being deserters, they could give it up and go home. Great men make wars; they also lose them. It would be spring soon and time for planting. The young boys, fourteen, fifteen and sixteen years old—and there were hundreds of them—wept now when they thought of their homes.

If the tall, skinny Virginian wept, he did so alone. Those who knew him well said that the only passion in his life was his lovely place at Mount Vernon. There are adventurers and there are householders; and those who imagined that Washington was an adventurer understood him very little. He knew every foot of his land, every board in his house.

There is a special kind of pain for the householder. When he goes away, he leaves a part of himself behind, and he is then split and filled with an aching desire for his home. He was not so different from the young soldiers. His was a homesick, broken and tired army.

His friend General Hugh Mercer was also a physician, a big, shambling man, who had studied medicine at Aberdeen

College and had once been a surgeon in the service of Charlie Stuart, pretender to the throne of England. Mercer came
to him with the table of sickness, and it did no good for
Washington to protest weakly that they were well enough
a few months before.

"They are not well now," Mercer said sourly.

Dysentery was epidemic in the camp; yellow jaundice,
or hepatitis, as we call it today, hundreds of swollen liv-
ers, colds, quinsy throat, pneumonia, venereal disease and
most of all a thing they called linenflame. This last was the
result of the fact that two-thirds of the army were clad
only in knee-length hunting shirts over knee-breeches. In
many cases, the knee-breeches had simply disintegrated,
leaving the men with only the shirts, their naked legs stick-
ing out below. They would tie around their legs whatever
pieces of cloth, blanket, felting they could get, but they
had nothing between their skin and the linen hunting
shirts. These shirts were made of tough linen that dried
poorly and slowly, and when it was wet for too long a
time—as it had been for the past two weeks— a nasty, itch-
ing deposit would form on the men's skin. They dreaded
this deposit and believed that it caused the ulcerated open
sores and the fever from which so many of them suffered,
as perhaps it did, for we have no exact knowledge of the
malady.

This and more Mercer specified, and he must have put
his medical problems to Washington as everyone else in the
army was putting problems with no solution to the commander in chief. It was one thing to pile the sick into wagons as you ran away; it was another thing to have them
here now with winter coming on. His total medication consisted of a few hundred pounds of Glauber's salts, and in

the entire encampment there was not a single set of bandages fit to use. Suppose they had to fight the British now? Would the wounded stop the bleeding with their own hands? Or would they simply bleed to death? There were no spirits, no oils—and the two dozen doctors who had remained with the army were being worked beyond endurance.

Washington was an antidote to anger and frustration. People who met him for the first time—having heard stories of his colorful language and towering rage in certain situations—were always astonished at the mildness of his voice and the gentleness of his manner, his blue eyes slightly perplexed, his attention fixed on every complaint or demand, no matter how small or pointless or potentially irritating.

He had heard from the Moravians in Bethlehem. Did Mercer know about the Moravians?

Didn't the general know that Bethlehem was forty miles away?

He knew that. At the same time, they had the wagons, and if the badly sick and wounded were put in the wagons and moved without haste, they could be in Bethlehem in less than three days. The Moravians were kind, good and generous people. They had a large functioning hospital, and they were willing to take the sick and wounded and feed and care for them.

Washington stressed that. The Moravians would feed the men, and the sick would be safe there, miles away from the center of action.

So each one had to be dealt with, and in the end it always came back to him. Not that his general officers were not good men; they were as distinguished and bright and interesting a group as one could find in any military establishment in the world—and more so, for most of them were civilians turned soldier, but only he could make the decision. Only he could decide whether the game was played out or not. The soldiers around their fires plagued their officers with questions: Do they build permanent quarters? Is this the winter encampment? Was the war over? Would they fight again, or would everyone go home? And the general officers plagued him.

His own calm covered a situation of chaos and madness. His quartermaster general was Thomas Mifflin, a successful Philadelphia merchant, and Washington called him in and told him that they needed a warehouse center for storage of food, clothes and ammunition, a central collection point. And Mifflin regarded him as if he were out of his mind.

Something in this manner: "Sir, we have no supplies to warehouse. We have no food. We have no ammunition. We have no clothes. What in God's name do we need a warehouse for?"

To Mifflin as to others, he stated his position very simply. An army without supplies cannot endure. He proposed to endure. Therefore, what was needed would be found. He was in the midst of a war, and he had no intentions of abandoning the cause to which he had committed himself. All this in very low key, for that was his way.

He had hardly awakened that first day in Pennsylvania before news was brought to him that the British had embarked an army in New York City and had set sail southward. Where to? Actually, to be landed on the Jersey shore, but Washington's first thought was of Philadelphia, and he wrote to Congress, simply and directly:

"There is not a moment's time to be lost in assembling

such a force as can be collected, as the object of the enemy cannot now be doubted in the smallest degree . . ."

He had lost an army. Very quietly, he announced his decision to assemble another one.

[14]

IT PRESSED UPON HIM hotly. Sunday afternoon on the eighth of December, he lay down for a little while in the bedroom at the Barclay house, and his servants tried to protect him. He was still in the clothes he had crossed the river with; but a messenger came, and young Hamilton, his aide, agreed that he must be awakened.

The messenger told Washington that General Howe's army had just entered Trenton—ten miles away—but was making no preparation to stay. Six, ten, fifteen thousand of them. The messenger was a spy or a patriot or an observer or a man out to make a dollar. Had he also informed the British that Washington was across the river? And with how many men?

How do you know he won't stay?

Because they pitched their tents in the meadows north of the town. Howe was riding the river bank with his staff.

Knox was there, in the crowded Barclay sitting room. Why weren't his cannon on the river?

They were.

Where?

Where they crossed, Knox told him—Knox, the fat, almost prissy young bookseller from Boston, who adored Washington—and must tell him now that there were eleven guns, no more.

Glover was there. Hell, no, he will not cross, was Glover's opinion. There were no boats on that bank, only hatred from the Jersey fishermen and ferrymen whose boats had been smashed to kindling.

The messenger wanted the center of attention again, and he said that there was enough sawn wood piled in Trenton to build a whole fleet of boats. Glover laughed. You don't build boats because wood is available; you need boat-builders. Anyway, the rumors were very strong that Howe would wait until the river froze over. Everyone had an opinion. There were other local people present, who had knowledge; but the messenger who brought the first news was paid off.

The commander in chief gave him money out of his own pocket and probably guessed that the man was taking money from the other side as well. That was the way it worked. For him, New Jersey was a land of spies, most of them double agents, hundreds of them moving freely in and out of the American and British encampments. Often enough, this movement was known by and earned the toleration of both sides. There had to be movement, buying and selling, purchase and delivery of supplies; allegiance was a fluid thing, and frequently the morning patriot became the evening Tory. Yet sometimes men totally identified with one cause or another attempted to move into an encampment, and sometimes they were caught and hanged, as Nathan Hale had been captured and executed by the British in New York City a few months before.

Still, they were paid. In those days particularly, Washington believed that their very existence depended to some extent upon knowing what the British were up to, and he

and his general officers paid spies out of their own pock-
ets—as indeed they paid for so many other things. Sometimes the information was true, and more often it was false,
but they always bought it.

Since the general had been awakened, William Alexander—the one so frequently called General Lord Stirling—
thought that he might talk to the men of the neighborhood.
They had come to wait upon him, and they were offering
their house. Truly, Washington wondered. He was very
moved at this. They were Quakers, most of them, by nature
for the rebel cause, men who were honored to take his
hand. He was now in their land, in Pennsylvania, which he
must accept as his own place. One by one, they introduced
themselves, Samuel Merrick, John Hayhurst, Robert
Thompson, Dr. Chapman, plain men plainly attired who
lived in the beautiful stone houses that stood on the gentle
knolls of Bucks County. Some of them he had met in
Philadelphia, and they reminded him of that meeting with
such sincere affection that tears came to his pale blue eyes.

[15]

MONDAY, ON THE NINTH OF DECEMBER, he wrote letters
with no address. When he wrote to General Gates, begging
him to come, he told the messenger that Gates was somewhere between the Delaware River and White Plains in New
York. And to General Charles Lee, he wrote:

"Philadelphia, beyond all question, is the object of the
enemy's movements, and nothing less than our utmost
exertions will prevent General Howe from possessing it. The
force I have is weak, and utterly incompetent to that end. I

must, therefor entreat you to push on with every possible succor you can bring."

The three thousand men with Lee and Gates had suddenly become the most desirable and wonderful fact on the face of the earth. He could play a game with what he had—as indeed he did—but above all he needed new men who were not sick and starved and broken.

He had already instructed his general officers to divide the men who remained on their feet into three categories: observers or sentries who would watch the bank; guards who would build little forts out of rocks and dirt and man these forts; and patrols, who had horses of one sort or another, or at least one horse to three men, and who would move along the river's edge. In a day's ride up and down the Delaware from where he was at Trenton Falls there were eight functioning ferries, Sherwood's, Coryell's, McKonkey's, Yardley's, Howell's, Kirk-bright's, Beatty's and the Trenton ferry. Earthworks at the ferries. He called to him the general officers whose brigades were in the best condition, Stirling, Stephen, Mercer and Fermoy, and told them about the ferries, the bank and Philadelphia, that they must hold the bank if the British tried to cross. Or die here.

To him, at least, everything had become simple, clear. The four men who faced him were as different from each other as four men could be. Lord Stirling claimed a Scottish title, more to irritate the British than for any other reason, although he appears to have had some legal right to noble rank. As William Alexander, he had been born in New York in 1726. When he was nine years old, his father, James Alexander, a fine lawyer, was retained in the Peter Zenger case and played an important part in freeing Zenger. All his life, William Alexander had been a civil libertarian, and it was a natural turn of events that made him into a rebel.

Adam Stephen, on the other hand, was a man described as having only two admirable qualities, his courage and the fact that he was a Virginian. He was quarrelsome, short-tempered and he drank too much. But he commanded a brigade of Virginia volunteers, 479 men, 70 officers, consisting of the 4th, 5th and 6th Regiments of Virginia Infantry, Washington's own people and those the commander felt were the most dependable soldiers he had.

General Hugh Mercer, at fifty-one, was much like a father to Washington, and the big, Scottish physician led five regiments of Connecticut, Massachusetts and Maryland Militia. Fermoy was a French soldier of fortune, whose brigade consisted of only two regiments, but both of them dependable, the Ist Pennsylvania and the Pennsylvania German Regiment, the Germans being as reliable as any soldiers in the army. As for Lord Stirling, his was a catch-all brigade of Virginia, Delaware and Pennsylvania volunteers.

But these were only a handful of soldiers, and they could accomplish little that could turn the tide. He needed a new army, and he told his secretary, Joseph Reed, to go to Philadelphia and find him five thousand men if he had to pick them up off the street.

Tall, charming, persuasive, Reed was a lawyer and a gentleman. He had been born in the little village of Trenton, across the river, and he knew every foot of this ground; and like Knox and Hamilton, he adored Washington. The pain of the dying army and its leader was his own. What should he tell them in Philadelphia, Reed asked, that the cause was dying?

Inform them that the need is very great—in effect Washington's summation of their condition. He became very soft of voice and very gentle when it was all stretched on a tight thread that the slightest shock might part. "Only find me men." The plea became a refrain. Old Israel Putnam, fifty-eight years old, the plainest of Yankees, a good farmer and a brusque and narrow man, old before his years, cruel and heartless, as some said, his whole body twisted with the pain of arthritis—even he had learned to respect this tall, slender aristocrat, George Washington of Virginia. Washington sent him to defend Philadelphia.

How?

Somehow, he told Putnam. Yet he needed men for himself. Reed would find the men; he might leave Putnam none at all. Yet he must defend a city that was indefensible. Mifflin would go with him to search for supplies.

Billy Smallwood, general of the Maryland Rifles, came to him. "Bullet stopper," they called him, so shot up that he could barely drag himself on crutches, with lead in his legs and his belly. It was his men who made up the smartest brigade in the army, one thousand Maryland Rifles, in long, fringed hunting shirts and white three-cornered hats. When they came marching through Philadelphia the year before, with fifty fifes playing and fifty drums beating, they were the proudest sight that city ever saw, as several citizens put it. Then they were caught in Brooklyn Heights by the Hessians, and 261 of them died there, pinned by bayonets when they could not reload their long rifles; and 200 more bore the wounds of that day. Now only 211 remained out of the original 1,000, and Brigadier William Smallwood came pleading to his commander in chief that he might be permitted to ride to Maryland and raise a new command, that surely there were a thousand more riflemen in Maryland who would rally to the cause and avenge all the fine lads who had died and whose corpses were rotting unburied in the woods in Brooklyn.

It must have been a moving scene, Washington telling him that he could not ride anywhere in his condition.

But he could. His good men lifted him onto his horse. The devil took his own legs; but he had the horse's legs.

Riflemen? Didn't he understand that riflemen were no good for fighting a war? Didn't he remember what had happened in Brooklyn and again in New York?

It was an accident. A rifleman was the finest fighting man on earth. His Maryland Rifles could hit a bee's eye at a hundred yards.

In the end, Washington let him go. It took two men to lift Billy Smallwood onto his horse, and off he rode to Maryland to find men for the army, his face full of pain and his heart full of hope. Yet he found some men, and came back not with a thousand but with a full hundred.

Perhaps the Virginian understood Smallwood full well. In a manner of speaking, he was wracked with his own pain; yet he had done what a man can do. If he had reached the bottom ground of his existence, it was not all bad; he had learned something about love and comradeship, and perhaps he was more content than we might imagine. He was defending his native land with no hope of gain, and the tedious argument of right and wrong that the politicians played was no longer his burden or concern. He understood the unexplainable, that the only holy ground is that place where a man lives and breathes, his mother the earth, which he must defend. The only award that still awaited him was either the loneliness of a British jail or the shameful ignominy of a gallows tree, depending upon the mood of those who pronounced sentence upon him. He was more imaginative than many of his friends believed, yet he could not conjure up any real hope of ever again being what he loved most, a peaceful householder in his beautiful home on the Potomac. The things that had mattered so deeply to him and which had made life a warm and generous thing, the riding to hounds, the designing of his gardens, the planting and transplanting, the gambling at whist, the flute that he practiced for hours behind closed doors—all of this was gone and most likely forever.

Yet he had a sort of repayment. He had stood face to face with eternity, and he was still alive and alert and surrounded by people who loved him.

[16]

WHEN OLD ISRAEL PUTNAM ARRIVED in Philadelphia on the next day, Tuesday, the tenth of December, he was told that carts were being loaded in front of the lodgings of practically every member of the Continental Congress—in spite of the fact that newspapers the same day carried indignant denials by Congress that it might be preparing to flee.

Putnam confronted them. Like so many men in the thirteen colonies, the members of Congress had a conviction that they were first on the British list of "those traitors promptly to be hanged." It was one thing for John Hancock to write his name so large on the Declaration of Independence that King George could read it without his glasses. That was in the warm summer days of July, when twenty thousand men stood to arms under the leadership of Washington; it was something else entirely in the cold December, with only a few thousand shivering men on the banks of the Delaware standing between Congress and the gallows. But then they were not alone in their self-esteem. Hundreds of others shared their conviction of a high priority on the British hanging list, and they demanded of Putnam what he intended to do.

He answered to the effect that he would do his duty.

Would he defend Philadelphia?

If it could be defended.

And if it could not?

Then he would do what a man could do, Putnam answered sourly. He would not run away. He had made his peace with the Almighty, and that was all that a man could do. Jehovah asked no more.

The congressmen felt that it was all very well to talk about Jehovah in Massachusetts or Maine, which was more or less His natural habitat, but this was Philadelphia. But Putnam would not be shaken. They would do well to unload their baggage. He would have no more talk of abandoning the city to the British. And he would like them to offer a substantial bounty for enlistments, for while it was all very well to talk about a man's patriotism, it never hurt to add a dollar or two to the persuasion.

[17]

GENERAL HOWE WENT IN and out of the village of Trenton in a hurry. He did not enjoy the Delaware River Valley, and he was rather annoyed that here in the Jerseys it should be colder than it was in New York City to the north, even though his weather experts told him that it was quite natural for the frost to settle into a river bottom such as this.

But New York was warmer in more ways than one. General Howe, who cherished women, found American ladies even more adorable than those he had left behind in England, particularly Mrs. Loring, blue-eyed, blond, gay, pretty, as addicted to cards as the general himself, and possessed of a most understanding husband. She became his mistress, his whist partner, and she kept his social schedule.

The rebels had fled New York City, for the bitter lesson of the young lad Nathan Hale, hanged for espionage in full view of the population, had driven home the fact that the city was occupied by a most determined enemy. Rebels who still remained slipped out of the town, especially those people of substance, leaving behind them a city whose "better people" were of one heart with the British.

Sir William Howe felt at home there, and on December II, he hastened back to New York, where Mrs. Loring's social book held a listing of six major balls, fourteen small but elegant dinner parties and any number of luncheons, which was not at all bad for a provincial capital.

In Philadelphia, not one ball. Even the flow of testimonial dinners for the members of Congress had dried up; the city was moody and depressed. And when Putnam and Reed decided that the Associators should leave the city and march up into Bucks County to join Washington, the city became even more depressed.

The Associators were an urban phenomenon. They had come into being with the Association, which had been set up in 1774 as a compact of merchants who agreed not to import, export or use British goods until the British were willing to redress the grievances of the colonies. Out of this had come a small volunteer movement of merchants, clerks, warehousemen, storekeepers, printers and other city folk who organized themselves into marching companies they called the Associators. There were about a thousand of these volunteers in Philadelphia, three companies of which—numbering about two hundred men each—Colonel Joseph Reed took north to Trenton Falls.

They were self-conscious city people, and they marched stiffly, for all of their training. But they had uniforms, brown trousers and blue coats, and they had real knapsacks and ammunition pouches and muskets. When they entered the American encampment, the bearded, long-haired regulars, clothed in rags and pieces of man-blanket and horse-blanket, stared at them dumbly. And Washington, so easily moved by kindness or help, was more disturbed than relieved. Here was the very life blood of Philadelphia city, given up to him, and he found that he could not in all conscience take these men away from the defense of the city. Instead, he put them under the command of Colonel John Cadwalader, with instructions to use these men to defend the river bank against a British crossing, from a point about ten miles south of Trenton down around the bend to Bristol, the part closest to Philadelphia that might still be crossed.

[18]

IN ALL TRUTH, Washington was puzzled, and he felt the desperate sense of entrapment that a blind man knows in a situation of grave danger. Not only were the two divisions of his army lost to him and apparently beyond contact, but he simply did not know what the British were up to. He had to know. Again he begged his general officers to buy information and pay the spies and informers whatever they asked, no matter how loathsome they appeared.

Howe had marched his Highlanders and his British regulars in and out of Trenton village, hardly pausing for breath. Were they back in New York, as some informants assured him? Were they boarding ship again for an attack on Philadelphia? Suppose they landed in Delaware by night; they could be in Philadelphia in three days. Then what was holding them back? Mrs. Loring? The tall Virginian loved women with as much delight as William Howe, but do you leave a dying army alone to diddle a married woman who's fair game for the field? Howe was no lovesick boy; he would not weigh a woman against a prize as rich as America.

Putnam rode up from Philadelphia and told Washington that the key to the whole thing was in the weather. It was the coldest December in anyone's memory, certainly in his, and anyone who knew the British realized that they would not march out against an enemy in weather like this. For one thing, they had no winter longcoats.

At least it was something Washington could have a good laugh over, even though he was not convinced. Putnam told him that the Continental Congress wanted to get out of Philadelphia. They felt that Philadelphia was an open city and could not be defended. They wanted to move on to Baltimore, which they held to be a safer place.

Nothing so far was as bitter as this. For them, for Congress, it was over then, and each man for his own neck. Philadelphia was only the financial, the manufacturing, the commercial center of the thirteen colonies; it was only the most vital of any city in America to the war effort, and at least three-quarters of the food and supplies that were now coming through to the army originated there or were transshipped through the city. Whatever small navy the Americans had was based there, and it was the largest and busiest port in America, the largest shipbuilding center.

Putnam repeated their demand. The Congress would not remain in Philadelphia; they were frightened. Better that he should suggest that Congress move to Baltimore than to have them scurry for safety, each to his own place, like hunted rabbits. That would be the end.

Very well, he told Putnam. Let them go to Baltimore.

So they did, without wasting an hour, and on the twelfth of December, 1776, they sent a message to Washington that said:

". . . that until they should otherwise order, General Washington should be possessed of all power to order and direct all things relative to the department and the operation of the war."

Well, he was now a military dictator of sorts. There appeared to be no end to the roles he would play.

[19]

THEN PART OF THE MYSTERY of what the British intended was solved. The British regulars left Trenton village; the Hessians marched in and occupied it, this time for the winter, settling down with the finality of men who had come to stay.

The first to arrive in Trenton were the grenadiers, some six hundred strong, led by Colonel Johann Gottlieb Rahl, who would be commandant of the entire occupying force. These men wore dark blue uniforms and sported great brass shakos, and they had the reputation of having killed more Americans than any other unit on American soil. They also were famous for their corps of trumpet, French horn and drums, often conducted by the colonel himself. He loved music, particularly military music.

The Knyphausen regiment followed Rahl's grenadiers, and they were in more or less the same strength, some six hundred strong. They wore black uniforms with silver facings, and almost every man in the regiment had a fierce black mustache, waxed and thrusting out horizontally, like two sharp sword points.

The two regiments took over the village methodically, in a practical and businesslike manner, but without any noticeable hostility toward those residents who had remained in their houses. About half of the village had fled; those who stayed, with some few exceptions, were Quakers, and their manner toward the Hessians was no different from the grave and courteous behavior they displayed toward anyone else.

Upon arrival, the Hessians posted notices around town:

SMALL STRAGGLING PARTIES NOT DRESSED
LIKE SOLDIERS AND WITHOUT OFFICERS,
NOT BEING ADMISSIBLE IN WAR WHO PRESUMES
TO MOLEST OR FIRE UPON SOLDIERS OR
PEACEABLE INHABITANTS OF THE COUNTRY,
WILL BE IMMEDIATELY HANGED WITHOUT
TRIAL AS ASSASSINS.

In all fairness, it must be stated that the Hessians hanged no one during their occupation of Trenton, nor did they inflict any cruel punishment that we have record of.

The following morning—Friday, the thirteenth of December—a company of fifty Jägers marched into Trenton, to join the two regiments already in occupation. The Jägers wore bright green uniforms with red facings and cocked hats. The Jägers were the Hessians most feared by the Continentals, perhaps because the German regiments in the American army had a traditional terror of the Jäger regiments in Europe.

In his own words, a Hessian appears far more human and understandable than as a historical memory, and what follows is an entry in a Hessian diary, made by one of the Jägers on the day they arrived in Trenton:

We marched to Trenton and joined our two regiments of Rall [sic] and Knyphausen, in order to take up a sort of winter quarters here, which are wretched enough. This town consists of about one hundred houses, of which many are mean and little, and it is easy to conceive how ill it must accommodate three regiments. The inhabitants, like those at Princeton, are almost all fled, so that we occupy bare walls. The Delaware, which is here extremely rapid, and in general about two ells deep [90 inches], separates us and the rebels. We are obliged to be constantly on our guard, and to do very severe duty, though our people begin to grow ragged, and our baggage is left at New York. Notwithstanding, we have marched across this extremely fine province of New Jersey, which may justly be called the garden of America, yet it is by no means freed from the enemy, and we are insecure both in flank and rear. The Brigade has incontestably suffered the most of any, and we now lie at the advanced point, that as soon as the Delaware freezes we may march over and attack Philadelphia which is about thirty miles distant.

In Trenton, as elsewhere, the ability of the Quakers to maintain themselves as they did during the Revolution is a testimony, not only to the Quaker faith, but to that quality so rare in war, compassion, which never entirely disappeared during the Revolution. The entire community of Quakers suffered uniquely during the war. Uncomfortably situated, poignantly conflicted by religion, ideals and principles, they were in their great majority entirely sympathetic to the American cause. Among many of them this sympathy was so deep-felt and profoundly religious, that in spite of their faith they took up arms in the Continental cause. But the majority of them adhered to their faith, bore the insults and taunts of both sides patiently and without bad will, and when the opportunity offered, provided food, shelter and medical aid to both the rebels and the British.

When the war began, the immediate reaction of Americans from those areas of the country where there were few or no Quakers was to regard them with suspicion and often with hatred and contempt. But as the war went on, these feelings changed to respect and admiration. The militant Protestant ideologies provided much of the impetus for the Revolution, and to religious people, the sense of the Quakers as Christians was hard to reject.

Yet, a Quaker meetinghouse was fair game for men who would think twice before defiling a church. Twenty members of the 16th Regiment of the Queen's Light Dragoons quartered themselves in the Friends' meetinghouse on Third Street in Trenton, filthied and damaged the place, and, on occasion, stabled their horses there.

[20]

ON SATURDAY, which was the fourteenth of December, one week after Washington led his beaten army across the Delaware, the Hessians completed their occupation of the little village of Trenton with the arrival of Colonel von

Lossberg's Fusilier Regiment. Their drums shattering the morning silence, their leggings chalked white, their coats bright red, they marched proudly into the village and quartered themselves in the Methodist and Episcopal churches. Later the same day, Colonel Rahl established his brigade hospital in the parsonage of the Presbyterian church. Dr. Elihu Spencer, the Presbyterian parson, was an avid book collector, and he complained afterward that the Hessians had used his books to light fires and to clean their boots.

With the arrival of the Fusilier Regiment of Hessians in Trenton, Sir William Howe completed his plans for the containment of Washington's shattered army until the Delaware River froze solid within a few weeks. He stationed his British troops in the rear, where they could easily join the Hessians when the time came for a general advance against the Continentals: a thousand Highlanders at Amboy, a thousand red-coats at New Brunswick and a thousand more at Princeton.

The Hessians—who were armed not only with their guns but with their reputations—were at the river bank itself, somewhat more than fifteen hundred men at Trenton and about the same number at Bordentown, some ten miles downstream and toward Philadelphia. Thus six thousand men were considered by the British as ample to deal with what remained of the American army. The rest of the troops were quartered in New York City for that interval—a short one they were certain—before the war ended.

THIS DESCRIPTION of the Hessian soldier is taken from Dunlap's *History of the American Theater:*

"A towering brass fronted cap; mustaches colored with the same material that colored his shoes, his hair plastered with tallow and flour, and tightly drawn into a long appendage reaching from the back of his head to his waist; his blue uniform almost covered by broad belts sustaining his cartouche box, his brass hilted sword, and his bayonet; a yellow waistcoat with flaps, and yellow breeches, met at the knee by black gaiters; and thus heavily equipped he stood as an automaton, and received the command or cane of the officer who inspected him."

The flamboyant, colorful, peacock dress of the Hessian soldier was by no means unusual in Continental Europe. There the uniform of the soldier had social as well as sexual—and often homosexual—significance. Its popinjay qualities were not without reason but served a very necessary purpose during the eighteenth and the beginning of the nineteenth century. Recruited most frequently from among the peasants, and often enough from the serfs, the Continental European soldier experienced a very significant change of character and position upon entering the army. From the very lowest rung of society he was elevated to a position of great subjective and even considerable objective importance; he was dressed in a colorful and striking uniform, and he was given the right to strut and parade his peacock feathers for the edification of the urban woman, whom he had always desired, even though she were maidservant or prostitute.

Criminal or peasant, he had once belonged to the least powerful element of society; now a musket was put in his hand and he was given the right, under certain conditions, to kill. This enlargement from subjugation to what was the ultimate power gave him a very distinctive and particular place in society.

The American soldier, on the other hand, was a world apart from this uniformed robot. Except for a few city companies of prosperous volunteers, the Continental had no other uniform during the year of 1776 than the clothes he wore when he had enlisted in the army either as a regular soldier or as a part of the militia. The whole symbolic significance of the uniform was lost upon him. Instead of the polished, bemedaled and brightly colored garments upon his own back, he saw them only upon the enemy and as a quality of the enemy. The popinjays were the others, not himself. He was recruited neither from the criminal classes nor from the serfs, but most frequently from the most advanced and educated elements of American society. What romance of warfare he might have gathered from storybooks had long since been dissipated by the bitter reality, and now soldiering in the army was to him and his fellows a common curse that had to be endured but never enjoyed. The only loyalty he had was to his cause, and this too was the only reason for existing as a soldier. He looked forward not to any rewards of cash, sex or plunder, but to that day when the unspeakable torment of the war would be over. Peace was paradise lost, the beloved condition in which he had once existed.

As for the Hessians, the American soldier despised them doubly. For one thing, they were the enemy; for another, they were foreigners who had been bought and paid for to

fight in a war that the American felt was as unjustly directed against him as ever an armed movement was unjustly
directed against defenders of their native soil. The English-
men were strangers from overseas who had come to take his
lands, burn his home, spoil his crop and put him into what
he considered profoundly—if emotionally—a condition of
virtual slavery; yet he could comprehend the motives of the
English, since he could remember them historically as owners of the country when they first took it for the Crown.

He had no such comprehension of the motives of the
Hessians; and along with lack of comprehension went the
ugly memory of what the Hessians had done to the raw,
unsoldierly, American boys on Brooklyn Heights and on
Manhattan Island.

[22]

GENERAL CHARLES LEE was a strange and misunderstood
man, who put himself outside of our history and outside of
some balanced comprehension of the situation in which he
found himself at the time. For that reason he was damned
beyond reason and perhaps beyond his deserving. Mrs.
Mercy Warren, a charming and perceptive woman of the
period, writing to Samuel Adams, said the following of Lee,
who was an acquaintance of hers: ". . . Plain in his person
to a degree of ugliness; careless even to unpoliteness; his
garb ordinary; his voice rough; his manners rather morose;
yet sensible, learned, judicious, penetrating."

He was not a man whom women found attractive.
Another woman of the time called him: "A crabbed man."
He was given to introversion, silences and too much alco-
hol, and he always resented the aristocratic airs of Wash-

ington and Washington's circle—unself-conscious though these airs might be—and felt that Washington's friends regarded him, an Englishman, as more renegade than recruit.

On December 12, he led his two thousand soldiers out of Morristown, New Jersey, and marched them eight miles to Vealtown, for what reason we do not know. It was in response to no commands or orders from Washington; nor was Lee such a person as to take others into his confidence. At Vealtown, he instructed General Sullivan, who was his second in command, to supervise the making of a temporary camp for the men.

Sullivan, an intelligent man and a lawyer, then thirty-six years old, followed Lee's orders only because he had a deep, ingrained respect for the military acumen of his commander. He knew all the unpleasant personal characteristics of General Lee, but at the same time he recognized Lee's incisiveness and his brilliance. In the year of war Sullivan had seen, he had experienced enough American blunders to make him slow to judgment and criticism, even though he knew Lee as an opportunistic soldier of fortune. In any case, they were not Lee's blunders. A profound supporter of the Continental cause, Sullivan had been a delegate to the First Continental Congress. He was at the siege of Boston, and he fought gallantly at the battle of Brooklyn Heights, where he had been captured by the Hessians. He was then exchanged for a British officer and was able to rejoin General Lee's command.

As far as we can gather, Lee looked at the few houses available around Vealtown and rejected all of them as "pious holes." The plain fact of the matter is that they were houses of Methodist and Lutheran families, and thus without liquor; and Lee wanted desperately to get drunk. He wanted to be away from righteous Americans.

Therefore he left his troops, taking with him only a guard of six mounted men, and rode to Baskingridge, three miles away, where he took up his quarters at the local inn. The amiable innkeeper at Baskingridge agreed that while General Lee could have a room upstairs, his six troopers must make their beds on the floor in the main room by the fireplace, a practice not unusual in those days and infinitely preferable to the open field.

Only minutes after Lee and his escort had left the encampment of the two thousand Continental soldiers at Vealtown, Major Wilkinson arrived with messages from General Horatio Gates to General Washington. Major Wilkinson was then nineteen or twenty years old—like other facets of Wilkinson, his age was hard to pin down—and from what others had to say about him, which was never laudatory, he was not an extremely trustworthy person. So far as one can put the pieces of his character together, he was a young man of opportunist tendencies and quick intelligence. As so often with men of that type, his ambition outran his store of common sense, and he all too frequently mounted the wrong horse at the wrong time.

On the other hand, he did subsequently write a journal of experiences in the Revolution, and the journal does provide a good deal of information that cannot be found elsewhere. Unfortunately the information, like the man, is not wholly to be trusted, and the central hero of whatever event described is always Major Wilkinson.

Wilkinson had been dispatched by General Horatio Gates who, with an army of between eight and nine hundred men, had been detained from joining Washington by an unseasonable snowstorm near the Wallpack River in New Jersey. His orders were to find Washington. It would appear that he had also been instructed by Gates to interview General Charles Lee and have an off-the-record discussion with him before he, Wilkinson, found the commander in chief.

Wilkinson rode from Gates's camp to Morristown, where he certainly had little expectation of finding General Washington but every expectation of finding Charles Lee. There he learned that Lee had gone on to Vealtown. Wilkinson rode there and spoke to General Sullivan and was now informed that Lee was spending the night at the inn at Baskingridge.

When Wilkinson got to Baskingridge, the inn was asleep. But he felt that his mission was important enough to awaken everyone in the house, and he hammered at the door. A sleepy innkeeper guided Wilkinson to Lee's bedroom. The night before Lee had had too much to drink, and now his response to being awakened was a furious outpouring, well-spiced with four-letter Anglo-Saxon words. It was the second time Lee had been disturbed that night. Earlier, a Tory had come to the inn to complain to Lee that a horse of his had been stolen from him by Continental army deserters. When Lee had cursed out the Tory roundly and thrown him out of the inn, the Tory swore he would get even.

Wilkinson, knowing nothing of the Tory incident, bore the abuse and delivered to Lee General Gates's letter, which had been intended for Washington. Apparently Lee was pleased to have a letter addressed to the commander in chief, and he read it immediately, without ever questioning the propriety of either Wilkinson's action or his own.

Lee refused to comment on the letter or to say anything about his own circumstances at the inn. Instead he told Wilkinson that he would see him in the morning light and that he should get the devil out of his room.

Wilkinson went down to the main room of the inn and spread his blanket in front of the fireplace, where several people were already sleeping, among them the six Continental soldiers who had come along from Vealtown as Lee's bodyguard. It was now about five o'clock in the morning. About an hour later, as the first hint of daylight came into the sky, five mounted Connecticut Militiamen rode up to the inn and banged at the door until they were admitted. They made enough noise to awaken Lee, and soon he came down into the main room of the inn, still in his slippers, with a coat over his wrinkled shirt. He was unshaven, and his shirt was dirty, so dirty that its condition was remembered and remarked upon not only by Wilkinson but later by the British as well.

Lee asked Wilkinson some questions about Gates's force, which Wilkinson had left not too long before. Wilkinson answered Lee's questions. Then Lee made some bitter and pointed comments about the lack of intelligence in Washington's movements, and he also commented unfavorably upon Washington's qualities as a leader.

The Connecticut Militiamen had been listening carefully. When they realized who Lee was, they approached him as a representative of Washington's staff and demanded back pay, forage and provisions. One of them also wanted his horse shod.

The Connecticut Militiamen were not a part of Lee's command, and certainly there was no way in which he could oblige their demands, but he represented the military authority and he was a general officer, and he was there.

Lee, British-born and educated, had no great love for Americans, but of all Continentals, he liked least the rustic Connecticut Militiamen, who were the opposite of his former British public school companions. Now he lost his temper completely and using his quirt drove the Connecticut soldiers out of the inn. Returning to the big kitchen, he continued to rage, his anger now directed toward his own guards, who were also New Englanders and possibly Connecticut men as well. Unwilling to withstand his fury or talk back to an officer, they slipped out of the inn and went around to the back of the building, facing the rising sun. There, wrapped in blankets, they sat and warmed themselves as best they could in the early winter sunlight and discussed their varying but similar opinions of General Charles Lee.

At this point, Colonel Scammel, who was second in command under Sullivan, arrived at the inn. Sullivan had sent Scammel to Lee for orders concerning the morning's march.

Lee listened absent-mindedly to Scammel, who could not quite disguise his reaction to the tall, skinny, dirty, pockmarked Englishman whose breath was sour, whose beard was of two days' growth and whose hair was uncombed and unwigged. Observing Scammel's attitude, Lee became petulant. What did Sullivan want of him? He had no maps. Had Scammel brought maps? How could he plan a march without maps?

Scammel had a map case on his saddle, and he went out to where his horse was tethered, got his maps and brought them to Lee.

Lee sat down with the map and traced with his finger a

route from Vealtown to Pluckamin, and from there eventually to Princeton. He then traced an alternate route from Bound-brook to Brunswick. He did this consciously as if he were performing for the people in the room, spelling out the routes for everyone to hear and follow his movements.

Both Wilkinson and Scammel knew full well that Lee's orders were to cross the Delaware at Alexandria and join General Washington. Here in this little company, three officers, an innkeeper and a waitress, Lee was parading his defiance of his commander in chief. He went on with this charade for a little while, and then he turned to Scammel and said sharply:

"Tell General Sullivan to move down toward Pluckamin; that I will soon be with him."

At this point Lee was intimating to Scammel and to Wilkinson that he would attack the British force at Princeton. Even if there had been some possibility of success in such a plan, the fact of his broadcasting it at the inn undercut and negated any element of surprise.

It was ten o'clock before Lee had properly dressed himself. Lee, Wilkinson and Scammel sat down together for breakfast, during which Lee could not refrain from a steady flow of caustic comments on Washington. The two younger officers listened quietly, and insofar as we gather from Wilkinson's memoirs, neither of them joined the attack on the commander in chief nor did they defend him.

After breakfast, Lee pushed the dishes aside, shouted for paper and ink and began a letter to General Gates. He had already arranged for Wilkinson to abort his mission of finding Washington and instead carry back with him to Gates Lee's own letter.

"The ingenious maneuver of Fort Washington," Lee wrote, "has completely unhinged the goodly fabric we had been building. There never was so damned a stroke; *entre nous*, a certain great man is damnedly deficient. He has thrown me into a situation where I have my choice of difficulties: if I stay in this province, I risk myself and my army; and if I do not stay, the province is lost forever."

While Lee was writing this letter, Scammel had mounted and was well on the way to Sullivan at Vealtown. Major Wilkinson, however, waited for the letter to be completed, so that he could take it back to Gates. He stood at the window of the inn overlooking the road, while Lee wrote.

We go back to the Tory Lee had thrown out of the inn the night before. Determined to revenge himself, this Tory rode eighteen miles through the night to the British encampment at Brunswick, where he gave them the information about Lee being at the inn. At first they were ill disposed to believe the man, but when he finally convinced them that a general officer of the Continental army was asleep and almost alone at the inn at Baskingridge, a Colonel Harcourt took a troop of dragoons and followed the Tory back to the inn.

As the dragoons approached the inn, Lee's guards, sitting behind the inn in the sunlight, saw them coming and guessed what they were after. They responded to the approach of the British by taking off across the fields as fast as they could run, their instinct for self-preservation larger than any desire to fight and die for Charles Lee.

Wilkinson was standing at the window. When he saw the British cavalry troop approaching in the distance, he shouted to Lee that British dragoons were there.

Lee, finishing the letter to Gates about Washington's inabilities, leaped to his feet and cried out, "Where?"

Wilkinson shouted that they were everywhere and in a moment would be all around the house. The letter was in Lee's hand, and Wilkinson snatched it and bolted. Lee began to shout for the guards and fired his pistols at the British and missed. The British were now in the house, and Lee was their captive.

Wilkinson claims in his memoirs that he drew his pistols and would have fought the British if there had been any hope of prevailing against a force of a dozen dragoons. But the fact of his escape makes it more likely that Wilkinson dived for the nearest hiding place and remained there until the British had departed.

In any case, Wilkinson must have hidden himself well, for the British took Lee, searched the house and rode off without ever finding him. Wilkinson claimed that the British shouted that if Lee did not surrender they would burn the house down, but this is at odds with the British account of the incident, which stresses the fact that they wanted Lee alive. They sought the great easy victory of capturing a Continental general, and here they got one of the four top general officers.

After the British had departed, Wilkinson saddled his horse and rode back to Vealtown to Sullivan's encampment. It was late in the afternoon when he arrived there, and Sullivan had already begun to march his men toward Pluckamin, in accordance with Lee's orders. Wilkinson told General Sullivan what had happened at the inn, and Wilkinson's excitement was such that he simply took it for granted that Sullivan, being second in command to Lee, would also be a part of the ripening cabal against Washington. Quite certain of this, he turned over the letter that Lee had intended for Gates to Sullivan.

However, Sullivan appeared to be undisturbed at the news of Lee's capture. He read the letter that Lee had written to General Gates without comment, returning it then to Wilkinson, suggesting that he take it along to Gates, for whom it was intended.

Wilkinson did not attempt to define Sullivan's attitude, but one can surmise that it was one of contempt. Sullivan then dispensed with Lee's orders, changed the direction of his march and set out to join his army to Washington's on the other side of the Delaware.

An hour later, Sullivan and his troops heard the British guns firing in celebration of the capture of an American general.

[23]

ON THE DELAWARE, as well as in the Jersey hinterland where Lee had been captured, the thirteenth of December was a frigid and dismal day, a mixture of rain and sleet. On the Delaware, the Americans were cold, despondent and miserable. In Philadelphia, the mood was one of impending disaster. A rumor raced through the town to the effect that General Washington and his staff had come to the decision to burn every building in Philadelphia to the ground, thereby providing no winter shelter for the British army. The reaction to this rumor by the citizens of Philadelphia, who so cherished their beautiful homes, was one of total dismay. A feeling of panic took hold of the city. The rumor appeared to be founded in fact, for the Congress had left Philadelphia the day before; and from the ragged army on the banks of the Delaware River came no note of hope or encouragement, nor was there any word in the newspapers of Lee's or Gates's army.

Early on the thirteenth, a messenger brought word of this harrowing rumor to the much-harassed General Washington, who immediately instructed General Israel Putnam to deny it emphatically. By the afternoon of the same day Putnam's heralds were reading aloud in Philadelphia the following statement of his military government:

"The General has been informed that some weak or wicked men have maliciously reported that it is the design and wish of the officers and men in the Continental army to burn and destroy the city of Philadelphia. To counteract such a false and scandalous report he thinks it necessary to inform the inhabitants who propose to remain in the city, that he has received positive orders from the honorable Continental Congress and from His Excellency, General Washington, to secure and protect the city of Philadelphia against all invaders and enemies. The general will consider every attempt to burn the city of Philadelphia as a crime of the blackest dye, and will, without ceremony, punish capitally any incendiary who shall have the hardiness and cruelty to attempt it."

Such was Israel Putnam's reputation for determination and for dedication to the cause he had espoused that any plot that might have existed to burn the city was quickly abandoned by the plotters. Philadelphia stood, in spite of the fact that everyone realized that its defense was impossible. There was no army to defend it, and neither was there at this moment any real determination among the leaders of the rebellion to defend Philadelphia, except for General

Washington and his staff; and even they were not wholly committed.

And the panic passed, particularly since the Council of Safety refused to abandon the city—as the Congress had—and remained in session, seriously considering every request from the army, no matter how unlikely it was that they could ever fulfill it. As for example the following plea from General Lord Stirling:

"You will please therefore, to forward to me immediately, such clothing as you have ready, to the number of two hundred and eighty suits. They want shirts, shoes, breeches, waistcoats, coats and stockings."

[24]

HOUR BY HOUR, the mystery of the whereabouts of Lee's army deepened—and Washington's hopes sank. On the fourteenth of December, Washington decided that somehow or other he must contact Lee, and he turned to his old and trusted friend, William Alexander, Lord Stirling.

Alexander was then fifty years old and not in good health. His joints were stiff with arthritis, and he was suffering a bad cold. Charitably, his drinking was an attempt to drown the pain of arthritis, yet there was rarely a night when he was not drunk—so long as his personal kegs of rum lasted. But he had once been surveyor general of New Jersey, and in that capacity knew every road and footpath in the entire state. The fact that he had a legitimate claim to a Scottish title led Washington to believe that perhaps Lee, always a snob, would be open to persuasion by him. Stirling, agreeing with Washington about the urgency and necessity of finding Lee's army, departed from the camp early on the fourteenth and rode north into Jersey.

As Washington had expected, his knowledge of the roads bore fruit, and before nightfall he met with Sullivan and the army on their way to the Delaware. Stirling then sent a mounted messenger back to Washington to inform him that the army was safe and whole and would join him very soon.

That morning, Washington had shifted his headquarters from Thomas Barclay's house to the home of William Keith in Makefield township, four miles north of Newtown, Pennsylvania. Washington considered this house to be better located in terms of the position of the army, stretched out as it now was in defense of the river bank.

The rate of desertion had increased, and on the same day Joseph Reed, Washington's secretary, sent the following plea to the Council of Safety in Philadelphia:

"It is of the greatest importance that all the arms should be taken from the soldiers who are leaving the army."

The arms were needed desperately, for the new recruits drawn from the Pennsylvania countryside were young farmboys, without guns. General Thomas Mifflin took the whole day of December 14 to visit every Pennsylvania village within a dozen miles of Washington's headquarters, holding meetings everywhere, pleading in each place for volunteers. As a result, about a hundred men were brought into camp.

Then Mifflin went on to Philadelphia, where he was able to persuade Colonel John Cadwalader to take a few hundred more of the Philadelphia Associators out of the city and lead them to the defense of the bank of the Delaware.

The Council of Safety, still in the city and still hoping

that the city would be closely defended, opposed this move. But both Washington and Cadwalader realized that if the river were once crossed by the British, any defense of the city would be impossible. Cadwalader informed Washington that the militia would indeed leave Philadelphia, and that evening Washington ordered him to lead the troops to Bristol and to join Colonel Joseph Reed there.

Before he went to sleep on the evening of the fourteenth of December, Washington had news from Stirling concerning Lee's army, but the account of Lee's capture was still very confused and the incident itself was surrounded by the wildest rumors.

[25]

ON SUNDAY, THE FIFTEENTH, Washington was still preoccupied with the desperate need to turn his sick, defeated and disorganized rabble into some semblance of an army.

He had already taken two sizable sections of his troops and assigned them to other parts of the river under the commands of Cadwalader and General Ewing. Now his attention focused on the problem of forming some sort of viable army under his own command. As yet the full possibility of such an army remained in the future, for Lee's troops under the leadership of General Sullivan had not yet arrived. Nevertheless, Washington knew they were on march toward his encampment, and he could begin the process of going through his own sick and dispirited forces to see what he might depend on.

So low had the fortunes of the Continental army sunk that at this moment, that is, on the day of December fifteenth, Washington could find no more than six or seven

hundred men whom he could place under his own command with the honest stipulation that they were fit for duty.

If we are to accept the fact that the core of the army consisted of those troops who were under his direct command
as Commander in Chief of the Continental Forces, then we
can comprehend the utter desperation of his position.

At this juncture the Virginian also faced the indignity of
being attacked by anti-Washington cabals made up of his
fellow Americans. *Cahal* is an interesting, old-fashioned
word that the dictionary defines as a small or restricted
group that is secretly promoting its own interest. Perhaps
because we live in an age when many groups promote their
own interests, the word *cabal* has fallen out of usage. But in
post-Revolution writing and discussion there were a great
many words written on the subject of anti-Washington
cabals. Perhaps the piousness with which such discussions
were framed is owing to the fact that Washington was so
early enshrined, robbed of all the human weaknesses that
underline the humanness of a man, and turned into an
improbable figure of unyielding stone and implacable
righteousness.

He was none of these things but a man facing defeat,
groping in a world of chaos for some sustenance, for some
way to retrieve his own fortunes and the fortunes of the
cause he led. His virtues were those one finds in a decent
and honest human being who, placed in awful circumstances, refuses to surrender to those circumstances.

In December of 1776, his failings were perhaps far more
apparent than his virtues.

". . . A motion had been made in that body [Congress]
tending to supersede him [Washington] in the command of
the army. In the temper of the times, if General Lee had

anticipated General Washington in cutting the cordon of the enemy between New York and the Delaware, the Commander in Chief would probably have been superseded. In this case, Lee would have succeeded him."

Wilkinson wrote this, and he was biased. Yet an element of truth exists in his observation.

Subsequent generations of historians have traced the beginning of a cabal in the motion mentioned above and perhaps rightly. All through December and perhaps through the preceding October and November, motions to replace Washington were made in Congress. Certainly there were groups in the Congress who regarded Washington with great distaste. There were equalitarian cliques, men whose thinking was shaped by New England historical circumstances and by a good deal of puritanism, who regarded Washington's way of life as deplorable. And there were other groups, of course, who felt that the situation wanted a professional military man, trained in Europe, of whom there were a good many, the two most outstanding being General Charles Lee and General Horatio Gates.

None of these resentments need have been a cabal, but they moved toward polarization and sectarianism. These were responses to the moment; for a lack of success brings with it a lack of confidence, and in all likelihood by December 16 General Washington's support in the exiled Congress was possibly less than lukewarm. There was also a tendency to blame Washington for the capture of Lee, for the congressmen refused to accept the fact that so brilliant and much-touted a soldier as Charles Lee could have walked into so silly and stupid a trap.

There were also some men in the Congress, supporters of Washington, who immediately leaped to the conclusion that Lee was a traitor and had been in cahoots with the British all the time and had betaken himself to the isolated inn in order to fulfill the conditions of a capture arranged in advance.

But there is absolutely no evidence in history for this kind of thinking, and the only explanation for Lee's capture is the foolish and petulant behavior that led him to it, although there is a serious question as to whether he did not enter into a treasonable arrangement with the British during or after his capture.

Washington at this point in his life gives one the impression of a man whose unwillingness to accept defeat has reached such proportions that if put to it, he will go on with the struggle with that handful of staff officers who were his close friends. On the sixteenth, he called a meeting of these staff officers, and out of this discussion came the proposal to empower all of his officers to recruit troops from the countryside and to promise a bonus both to those who raised the troops and to the new soldiers.

There was no money to draw upon; and to this extent the plan was dubious, although Washington and a number of his officers had in the past paid military expenditures out of their own pockets.

At this time Washington could have done as he wished, for he had sufficient dictatorial powers granted to him explicitly by the Congress, and in other instances relinquished to him by tacit surrender of responsibility by many people in official positions. Yet he could not break himself of his daily habit of reporting to those he continued to consider his civilian superiors and to the private people to whom he felt he had a debt of responsibility. Thus he wrote to Congress on December 16th, concerning his emergency recruiting measures:

"It may be thought that I am going a good deal out of the line of my duty to adopt these measures or to advise this freely. A character to lose, and a state to forfeit, the inestimable blessings at stake, and a life devoted, must be my excuse."

Pleading, begging, entreating—these were attitudes foreign to Washington—yet here on the sixteenth of December, he is at one of the very lowest moments of his existence.

After he had finished his letter to Congress, he wrote another letter to his brother Augustine, of whom he was very fond, and to whom he felt he could turn in his worst moments. He told his brother of the circumstances of Lee's capture and then added: "the more vexatious, as it was by his own folly and imprudence, and without a view to effect any good, that he was taken."

This is about as severe as Washington's public criticism of Lee was at the moment. About a year later, under very different circumstances, Washington would launch a stream of direct and personal invective at Lee almost beyond description, but that would be in the heat of the Battle of Monmouth and understandable under the circumstances.

In the same letter to his brother Augustine quoted above, Washington added:

"If every nerve is not strained to recruit the army with all possible expedition, I think the game is pretty nearly up. You can form no idea of the perplexity of my situation. No man, I believe, ever had a greater choice of evils and less means to extricate himself from them."

So desperate was Washington's situation that he instructed all brigade commanders to plead with their troops for six weeks more of service, that is, with those whose enlistments were expiring daily. He ordered them to promise such troops a bounty of ten dollars for the six weeks, but he had no money outside of his personal funds with which to pay them. He was prepared to pawn all he owned to meet this obligation. At the same time, he promised an increase of their pay by twenty-five percent.

If he were forced to carry out both these promises, it could result only in his own financial ruin. His behavior here is much like that of a man so close to destruction that he feels that nothing he does to survive can be subject to criticism.

One crumb of sustenance was offered to General Washington before the wretched day of December 16th was finished. General Sullivan and Lord Stirling had brought Lee's army across the Delaware to the west bank at Easton. From Easton, Sullivan sent a messenger to Washington. The messenger arrived at Washington's headquarters at the Keith house late on the sixteenth.

When he went to bed at long last on the sixteenth of December, Washington knew that Sullivan's troops were safe in the momentary security of Pennsylvania.

[26]

THE CONTINENTAL YANKEE—and perhaps his descendants as well—had a penchant for exaggeration and a hopeless fascination for the profession of spying. Perhaps because never before had they found a product so easy to merchandise and so simple to create as information, and when they weighed the small, mean reality of actual information against the grand splendor of manufactured intelligence, they appeared always to choose the latter. A shrewd and equivocal Yankee—and they existed in abundance—knew full well that if he entered a British encampment and sold them the story of two Continental deserters on their way home, it would fetch him most likely a kick in the pants or a whip across his back in payment. On the other hand, if he turned the two deserters into a full column and changed the direction of their march so that it made sense, the information was worth a shilling at least. A full regiment on the march for forage or horses or to set up an ambush was worth a half-crown, and a brigade marching to attack might fetch a full pound.

But in the latter case, he had to be careful, for the British were likely to hold onto him until they had a chance to test his story and then take back their pound and give him a good beating in the bargain.

So the Yankee merchant of information preferred to deal in small tidbits, which he sold to both sides. He found that a base of reality was preferable to total invention, and if he sold information about a battery of eighteen pounders, he felt more certain of his ground if he had actually seen at least one five pounder.

On the tenth day after Washington and his broken army had reached the Delaware River and crossed it—that is, on the seventeenth of December—neither he nor the British knew what he intended. For Washington, the future was desperate and bleak; the enlistment period of three-quarters of his army was running out, and in exactly two weeks the

Continental Army of the Thirteen American Colonies would cease to exist as a meaningful or viable force, that is, considering that nothing of great moment happened. And the only contingency that held promise of great moment, a victory over the British, was hardly even a vague possibility. Yet, he had to move or perish.

Washington knew this. Major General Sir James Grant, whom Howe had left in command of the containing force, and whose headquarters were at New Brunswick in Jersey, knew this—and practically everyone in New York, Philadelphia and all the country in between was aware of it. It was the greatest heyday for the information market that America had ever seen, and since it was winter time, with neither plowing nor reaping to be done, practically every other farmer, tradesman, merchant and peddler in New Jersey became a part-time spy.

The market was good. Both Grant and Washington bought everything offered with a sense of desperation. Washington had to know what Grant intended to do, and Grant had to know what Washington intended to do. The British paymaster had what was euphemistically called an "information fund"; Washington and his general officers paid out of their own pockets.

To this point, the following exchange of letters is most interesting, both as to the quality and amount of information sold.

The letters moved between General Grant and Colonel von Donop. There were two encampments of Hessians on the Delaware River during that December, one at Trenton under the command of Colonel Rahl and the other at Bordentown under the command of Colonel von Donop. The first message is from Von Donop to General Grant, and dated the seventeenth:

In accordance with my communication of yesterday, I have the honor to advise you, my General, that the patrol has been sent out and seen nothing of the enemy. They found near the bridge between Mount Holly and Morristown a quantity of cannon ball and shells which they threw into the water. According to the reports of the country people the enemy must be at Coopers Creek with a force of four thousand men and General Putnam who commands them must be busy in collecting stores. If I did not know that the heavy artillery were to arrive today or tomorrow I would be very desirous of marching with three batallions and making a call on Mister General Putnam. I will follow out your orders on this subject as soon as possible. Yesterday evening a farmer came to say that General Washington had crossed the river at Vessels' Ferry* with a large force on the right flank of Colonel Rall [sic] for the purpose of uniting with the corp of General Lee. The man however has disappeared after telling his story to the Mayor of Burlington. If this news is true the troops which have crossed must be the corp of General Stirling, who has his quarters at Beaumonts about two miles above the ferry. The six chasseurs who were lately driven from the house near the river at Trenton were again attacked yesterday morning by a detachment of the enemy which crossed in three boats under the protection of the eighteen pounders in their batteries. We were not able to prevent them from landing and were obliged to retire until Colonel Rall [sic] brought up a force to their assistance. After this the rascals went off taking away as their only prize a pig which had just been killed by the Chasseurs. The two which came near me here and

*Vessels' Ferry, as the British called it, is the same as McKonkey's Ferry.

which I made mention of yesterday, I believe have gone down the river to await me at Burlington. I have the honor to send you two orders issued by General Putnam. It is evident that we will have to make a siege of it. At this moment I have just received the news sent yesterday evening of a patrol of six dragoons to Pennington, which has not yet returned and one of these dragoons has been seen ten miles from Trenton mortally wounded.

The above communication is fascinating both because of the valid intelligence and misinformation the Hessian commander had obtained. Putnam commanded no force of four thousand men, nor was he at Cooper's Creek. The news that he received from a farmer that General Washington had crossed the river to join the force of General Lee was utterly without foundation. Either the farmer was peddling manufactured information, or he had enough wit to mislead the enemy. Even the mention of General Stirling's quarters is incorrect, for on that day General Stirling was quartered in the Thompson-Neely house. As for the eighteen pounders that the Continentals purportedly had across the river near Trenton, this was the most interesting of the fictions. Not only did the Continental army have no such guns on either the east or the west bank of the Delaware River, but they would hardly waste their small and precious store of ammunition throwing cannonballs aimlessly across the river.

On the same day, General Grant replied to Von Donop, dating his letter Brunswick, seventeenth December, 1776:

I have just received your report of this day's date . . . I could hardly believe that Washington would venture at this season of the year to pass the Delaware at Vessels Ferry, as the repassing it may on account of the ice become difficult. I should rather think that Lee's corp has proceeded to Philadelphia, for we have heard nothing of them, since Lee was made Prisoner, and prior to that the intention was to march to East-town in order to cross the river.

Putnam's handbills and Lee's account differ exceedingly about the intentions of the Rebels with regard to Philadelphia. For Lee declared that they are determined to burn the Town, if they cannot prevent its falling into our hands. General Matthew marched this morning to Plackhemin where he fell in with a small body of rebels; they fled on his approach—he had taken a few prisoners—Some Arms and stores, his guide was wounded in the foot, that was all the loss we sustained. General Leslie marched this morning to Springfield and is to proceed from thence by Bound-brook to Prince Town. I have had no report from him, and cannot expect any until tomorrow.

It can be seen from the above that General Lee talked freely after his capture and that he had been privy at least to the plans of whatever party in Philadelphia was promoting the notion of burning the city. One should not confuse the suggestion of burning Philadelphia to the ground with the modern strategy of the scorched earth. There was no question of scorched earth or of putting the British into a position where they faced a severe winter with no shelter. Already they were in occupation of New York City, and housing there was ample for all of their needs. Apart from this, there were a hundred hamlets such as Trenton that they could occupy. The burning of Philadelphia was the sort of grotesque plan that grows out of desperation, shortsightedness and the kind of hysterical necessity that must effect something of a dramatic nature regardless of what the incident might accomplish.

It is also interesting to note the overestimation of the Continental forces by the British. The British were never able to forget their first taste of American warfare during their bloody retreat from Concord and afterward at the Battle of Bunker Hill outside of Boston. The horror of the awful toll taken of them there lingered, and even though they were able to inflict defeat after defeat upon the Continental army, they were not willing to give up completely their initial picture of American power and determination.

[27]

SITTING IN THE KEITH HOUSE, his new headquarters, on the eighteenth of December, 1776, General Washington watched a light snow fall from a dark sky and penned one of the saddest notes of his career. Addressing himself to the Pennsylvania Council of Safety, he wrote:

"Your collection of old clothes for the use of the army deserves the warmest thanks."

The snow drifted down, and the Americans shivered and waited. They were on the west bank of the river, and they were alive. Being there meant that they must try to keep warm and to stay fit; and since it was a cold day, they huddled in their shelters and counted the hours to the end of their enlistments. The officers quartered in the various houses along the river huddled around their own fires, and in these homes there was little joy, no celebration, no yuletide cheer and very little willingness to contemplate a future that offered nothing.

Across the river at Bordentown, on the same day, Colonel von Donop wrote another letter to his superior, the British General Grant, apologized for his overestimate of Putnam's strength in his letter of the day before, and went on to say:

"Sir: I have this moment received your letter of the seventeenth instant. Since I had the honor to advise you that there was four thousand of the enemy at Cooper's Creek the best report I can obtain reduces the number to Five hundred. I do not care to take the trouble to march with all my force for these gentlemen will not wait for me."

Indeed, if there actually were five hundred Continental soldiers on the east bank of the Delaware—something that cannot be verified now and which appears quite impossible—they certainly would not have waited for Colonel von Donop and his Hessians.

On this day, a Mr. Smith arrived from Philadelphia. Mr. Smith moves through history facelessly, only known by his family name, which is recorded in the Hessian notes. He brought information from Philadelphia to sell to the Hessians, and since the information would have to contain enough drama to earn its price, he told Colonel von Donop that the people in Philadelphia were "hard at work fortifying the city."

However, another informant told Colonel von Donop: "From the way they are doing it, the work will not be finished in two years," which was less dramatic but more truthful.

By the eighteenth of December the Hessian commanders were beginning to satisfy themselves that no enemy worth their apprehension or their effort still existed on the west bank of the Delaware River. During the next three days they would reinforce that observation, and by Christmastime they would be willing to write off the Continental army entirely.

[28]

FOR TWO WEEKS, the mood of the people of Philadelphia had been one of total despair concerning the cause for independence and the security of their city. On December 19, however, the Pennsylvania *Evening Post* cheerfully published the following:

"There is no doubt that the enemy will be repulsed with great slaughter, if they should attempt to cross the river."

This kind of boastful confidence was not actually founded in reality, but it was helped by the publication on the same day, December 19, 1776, of Thomas Paine's first *Crisis* paper.

Thomas Paine had been with the American troops all through the month of November, during their retreat through New Jersey and most likely up to the point of their first crossing of the Delaware River from east to west. It is difficult to ascertain what position he held during that period. Some of the men on that march suggest in their memoirs that he was brevetted an officer of sorts, and this is just possible, so loosely were officers made and unmade then. Washington took a great liking to Paine; and the two of them, Washington and Paine, spent many hours discussing the meaning and the direction of the war. Paine informed Washington that he would attempt to write something that might help the army, and Washington was enthusiastic about his project. They both shared a sort of mystical faith in the power of the printed word, and the astonishing success of Tom Paine's book, *Common Sense*, had left every literate person in America with the feeling that somehow Paine's pen could perform miracles.

This was hardly the case, and it is doubtful whether, after the November retreat of the American forces, even a miracle would have changed the depressed mood of the defeated soldiers.

However, when Paine left the troops at the Delaware, he had already written some pages of manuscript. Legend has him sitting among the shivering troops in the light of a campfire, writing down the words of the first *Crisis* paper. But the greater likelihood is that he only jotted down notes of the retreat—as so many others did—and actually wrote the *Crisis* in Philadelphia.

There, he had it printed in a Philadelphia weekly, the *Pennsylvania Journal*, and the first bundle of newspapers came off the press either late on the eighteenth of December or perhaps very early in the morning of the nineteenth. In any case, on the morning of the nineteenth, Paine had a rider load his saddlebags with copies of the newspaper and gallop off post haste to the encampment. The rider must have left sometime before dawn, because Washington had the first *Crisis* paper in the morning and read it through at luncheon on the same day. There is evidence that Washington was thrilled with what Paine had written, for he immediately ordered copies of the *Pennsylvania Journal* distributed up and down the river to every brigade, with instructions that it be read aloud at each corporal's guard.

"These are the times that try men's souls. The summer soldier and the sunshine patriot will, in this crisis, shrink from the service of his country, but he that stands it now, deserves the love and thanks of man and woman."

It echoed and reechoed up and down the frozen bank of the Delaware, until there hardly was a man in the Continental army who did not know the words; and all things considered, there certainly must have been some who detested them. Paine's first *Crisis* paper, of course, has increased in stature with the passing years, but one can hardly imagine that the reiteration of platitudes to the bitter, defeated army of shivering and hungry men on that winter day gave them any great purpose or passion.

Washington's old, good friend, General Hugh Mercer, had been doubling as a physician, and since the crossing of the Delaware on the seventh of December, sickness had increased. Rash, dysentery, jaundice—apparently there was no end to it. On the same day, December 19, while Tom Paine's words were being read aloud at the corporal's guard, General Mercer wrote to Joseph Blewer, the secretary of the Philadelphia Council of Safety: "With regard to my people's sleeping, we have only three rugs and three blankets . . ."

So to all effect and purpose, it had come to an end. The fine and grand volunteer Continental army had run headlong into the brutal animal game of war, and it had been defeated and shattered. The braggarts, the vainglorious, the loudmouths, the thieves, the cutthroats—all those who come together out of the heady variety of a nation when some great common project is under way—all had deserted; others were in the British prisons or had died, and still others packed the hospitals with their wounds and scurvy and disease.

The officers began to turn surly and to take it out on the men, and the Connecticut dowsers predicted the worst winter in years and the days grew shorter and bleaker, until the solstice was only two days away.

So the first part of the crossing was finished.

THE SECOND CROSSING

CROSSING

West to East

[1]

ALEX SCAMMEL WAS a Harvard graduate, then a schoolteacher and then a surveyor. He was over six feet tall and very good-looking and possibly vain of his hair, which he wore long and ribboned at the back. He had been in love with Abigail Bishop of Medford, Massachusetts, and when she wouldn't have him, he lost all interest in the law he was reading in John Sullivan's office; and when Sullivan said to him, "I'm closing up the office because other more important things have come up," Alexander Scammel replied that he was with him all the way. Sullivan became a brigadier, and Scammel was given a colonel's rank over the 3rd Massachusetts Continentals. It did not matter that Sullivan was a lawyer and Alex Scammel a teacher, because the soldiers they led were no more soldiers than they were officers.

However, time had its way with the lot of them, and when Sullivan took command of the army—after Lee had been captured—Alex Scammel became his immediate aide and second in command. Scammel had turned into a good leader, and the 3rd Massachusetts was one of the most effective regiments in the army.

Sullivan had marched his men almost on the double since Lee's capture; they were exhausted after crossing the river, and Sullivan rested them while he sent Scammel riding down to McKonkey's Ferry to see what the Virginian desired.

Washington's headquarters were at the Keith house, but as often as not he centered his affairs and his command post at McKonkey's. For one thing, McKonkey ran a public house; and if a hundred men in wet boots and dragging spurs clumped in and out in the course of a day, well, that was what the house was for, and Old Man McKonkey liked the trade, not only for the money it brought but because he was heart and soul a rebel. He was flattered with the big Virginian and all the other fine gentlemen giving him their patronage, and since he had never catered to so genteel a trade before, he could never quite get over their courtesy. He took to bowing to ladies and changing his shirt twice a week.

Washington liked Scammel and asked him how the men were. He wanted the truth.

Well enough, Scammel replied.

Washington said that they were all well enough, since they were still alive. But how well? How many sick?

There were less than a hundred in carts, Scammel replied. The rest were walking.

Clothes?

Charlie Lee, Scammel began.

Charlie Lee—no, the commander in chief frowned. General Lee. He was still a general officer.

He had made them wash their clothes every fortnight. General Lee had commandeered eleven hundred jackets with scrip. Most of the men had shoes. There were four

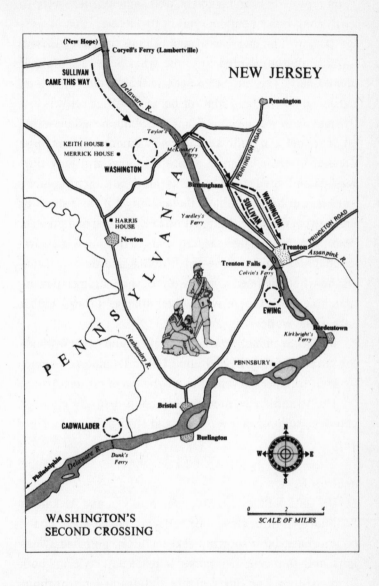

Coryell's Ferry (Lambertville)

NEW JERSEY

SULLIVAN
CAME THIS WAY

Delaware R.

Pennington

KEITH HOUSE
MERRICK HOUSE

Taylor's

McKonkey's Ferry

WASHINGTON

Birmingham

PENNINGTON ROAD

Yardley's Ferry

WASHINGTON

SULLIVAN

HARRIS
HOUSE

Newton

PRINCETON ROAD

Trenton

Assanpink R.

P E N N S Y L V A N I A

Trenton Falls

Colvin's Ferry

EWING

Neshaminy R.

Bordentown

Kirkbright's Ferry

PENNSBURY

Bristol

CADWALADER

Burlington

N

Delaware R.

Dunk's Ferry

Philadelphia

W   E

S

0   2   4

SCALE OF MILES

WASHINGTON'S
SECOND CROSSING

hundred Rhode Island soldiers, and some of them were so seedy they walked barefoot out of preference, even in winter time, with no more sense about things than a red Indian.

Washington wanted to know what Scammel thought about Charlie Lee, and Scammel said that he didn't like him, but he could not fault him for being an officer. It was just the man who was lacking. Then Washington said he wanted Scammel and Sullivan and every damned officer to be dressed in clean linen as white as snow, and how they washed and dried it out in this weather was their problem, not his; but he would have them skinned if their shirts or jabots were dirty. He wanted uniforms stitched and pressed, no torn coats, no bare heads. He wanted them in wigs, powdered, boots blackened, swords shining, and then he wanted the whole damned army, two thousand strong, to come marching down the Delaware River Road as if they hadn't a care in the world.

And as Scammel regarded him incredulously, Washington asked, did they have drums? Fifes? Trumpets?

Four trumpets, seven fifes, maybe twenty drums.

The Virginian wanted music, good, bad—he couldn't care less, so long as it was loud and strong.

[2]

SO ON DECEMBER 20, 1776, John Sullivan and Alexander Scammel—both in clean shirts, decent coats, black boots, cocked hats, both sporting real epaulets, polished sword hilts, both prancing their horses in real smart style and both followed by a fine flurry of fife and drum—led two thousand Continental troops who came marching to join the army on the Delaware. General Washington had lined up his own men along the road, and when Sullivan's troops came stepping smartly along, the Continentals broke into the first heady cheer in many a long month, yahooing and yelling "Razza-doodle-doo for Rhode Island!", for there were four hundred smart Rhode Island lads, all in knee-length hunting shirts, all of them armed with big Brown Betsys, the English-made muskets that couldn't shoot straight but held a long bayonet.

And then there was a surprise. Sullivan and Scammel were grinning as they watched the tall Virginian as he stood up high in his saddle and saw behind Sullivan's two thousand men, eight or nine hundred more, led by General Horatio Gates and Colonel Benedict Arnold. They had all come in together, and now his own Continentals broke ranks, screaming; and Sullivan's men and Gates's men also broke ranks. And there was embracing and wrestling and kissing and weeping, as brothers and cousins and even fathers and sons found each other.

Washington's own eyes were wet, and he could not have spoken then. He had three thousand more men in his army now, and the news ran like wildfire, south to Philadelphia and Baltimore, and north to the British. The agent was Mr. Hovenden, and he reported to the British:

That the main body of the army lies at Beaumonts between Telits and Baqers ferry about eleven miles above Trenton ferry commanded by General Washington and Lord Stirling. That a party of about three thousand men under General Sullivan had joined General Washington and it was said that they were imme-diately to march and make their quarters at Newtown. That of this number more than two hundred sick and wounded invalids were arrived at the hospital at Newtown. A party of two hundred or three hundred men are stationed at Robinsons ferry about seven miles above Beaumont. Dont know of any other party higher up the river. That General Washington had with him six eight pounders but were removed from thence, know not where. They are opposite to Slacks Island and about five miles below Beaumonts four eight pounders. That below Slacks Island and at Yardley's are about six hundred men, commanded by Gen. Dickinson, with two pieces of cannon. Gen. Mercer was there but often shifts his quarters. That upon the most diligent inquiry and best intelligence he can procure, General Washington's army did not consist of more than eight thousand men. That General Sullivan went to Philadelphia on the Fifteenth inst. from Washington's quarters. General Gates had not passed the river on Thursday last, but was informed, that he was coming forward with about five hundred men.

Half true, half out of whole cloth. But that was what was sold and what the British bought.

[3]

LIKE GENERAL CHARLES LEE, General Horatio Gates was a British officer who had joined the American cause. He came of a better background—that is, in British class terms of the time—than did General Lee. General Lee. Born in Maldon, England, in the year 1728, he was a godson of Horace Walpole. Though he was the son of a household servant, he was raised as an English gentleman, more or less in the bosom of the British army. He was wholly a product of the British army, enlisted by his parents when still a boy and achieving, finally, the rank of major. Sent to America during the French and Indian War, he fought with Braddock and was severely wounded in 1755. Recovered from these wounds, he joined the British expedition against Martinique in 1762. However, he was poorly rewarded in the British army; disgruntled, a plotter, a man who could get along with almost no one, Gates, like Charles Lee, would constantly create for himself untenable situations.

One such situation made him decide to move to America permanently, and he purchased an estate in Virginia. Whether his sympathies were with the Continentals or simply against the British, it is hard to say; but when the Revolutionary War broke out, he immediately offered his services to the Continental army.

The War Committee of Congress was thrilled with the opportunity of having a professional soldier of Gates's stature; and some time in June of 1775, they appointed him adjutant general of the Continental army, carrying with it the rank and pay of brigadier general. In such circumstances, it was inevitable that he would see himself as the first rival to General Washington for the command of the army, and from the very moment of Washington's appointment, Gates felt that he himself had been overlooked and slighted. Like Lee, he had small opinion of Washington's military capabilities, and again like Lee, he had an equally small opinion of the courage or capability of the American soldier.

By December of 1776, both Gates and Lee had surrendered any hope of a victory by the Continentals; it would appear they were both thinking of how to bargain to the best advantage with the British. And certainly, when General Horatio Gates arrived at the encampment on the banks of the Delaware River, he saw no possibility of retrieving the fortunes of the defeated army.

On the other hand, Washington welcomed Gates's

arrival, relieved that he had a military man of his experience and stature to replace General Lee. In a world where malice is omnipresent, it is difficult to understand someone without it. The humility of a meek man is far more comprehendible than the humility of a proud man like Washington, who had qualities of enormous strength and unshakable will. These qualities he combined with gentle demeanor that misled people into thinking that he was either a fool or a bungler.

In this manner of gentleness, he turned to Gates because he felt that Gates might help and advise him.

[4]

PERHAPS HE ALSO TURNED to Benedict Arnold, but this we don't know; nor is there anything to indicate what happened between him and Arnold except that Arnold saddled his horse and rode out of the encampment, ostensibly to go to Boston and recruit men. But from there to Boston in even the best of weather was two weeks by horse, and in three days less than two weeks, the game would either be played differently or past any playing at all.

Washington had come to the decision that it must be played differently, and for days he had been turning over in his mind a scheme he had and perhaps passing a word or two about it to those two friends upon whom he depended so much, Hugh Mercer and William Alexander. But not to anyone else; mouths were bitterly tight about this, for when it came to the end of something, there was no one to trust, and men marching together to the gallows put a cheap price upon each other.

But he would put his scheme to Gates. Wasn't everyone

saying that Gates was the most brilliant military man in North America, and did they not group him always with Cornwallis? No one placed the Virginian with Cornwallis. Washington was still very much the civilian, the husband-man; the man who could ride through his garden and name every shrub, when it was planted or transplanted; who worried about a sick colt and approached every game of whist with excitement and some trepidation. Gates was the *pro*; Washington was the pretender.

Gates was also a British gentleman, and that night at the Keith house, Washington begged the Keiths' indulgence for a dinner for two with his own silver and his own cloth and plate. And he sent his servants to find a decent piece of meat, turnips, parsnips, carrots, cheese, whatever the camp would yield that wasn't camp food, for it had to be the best for Gates.

Perhaps then at that moment, Washington believed even less in himself as he watched Gates react to his somewhat primitive Continental elegance, there in that cramped stone house that was his headquarters. Surely Gates must have known what was coming, and possibly Gates was certain in his own mind that the approach of the commander in chief would be as witless as he had anticipated.

Then, the meal done, the second bottle of wine opened, Washington took him into his confidence. The plan was very simple and very direct. Washington proposed to Gates that they take all the forces at their command on the west bank of the Delaware River, plus every available man out of the Philadelphia Militia; that they divide these available forces, which numbered almost six thousand men fit for action, into three brigades, and that simultaneously the three brigades cross the Delaware River at three separate points and attack the Hessian outposts at Trenton and at Bordentown. He, Washington, would cross with one force at McKonkey's Ferry, which was about nine miles above Trenton, and from that place he would march down the river on the east shore to attack Rahl's encampment at Trenton. General Ewing with as many of the Pennsylvania Militia as could be put under his command would cross about a mile below Trenton. Arriving at their landing place, they would then march north and secure control of the stone bridge over the Assanpink Creek, which was a brook flowing along the south side of Trenton. From that position they could cut off any retreat of the enemy to the south while Washington's army attacked in force from the north.

The third part of the plan proposed that Colonel Cadwalader take all of the troops that were now guarding Philadelphia and cross the Delaware River below Burlington. From there, they would attack the southernmost Hessian encampment under Count von Donop. The plan was not yet fully composed. But in a general sense Washington knew exactly what he wished to do. He felt that the Hessians were secure in their encampments, that they were not expecting any attack, and that such an attack might not only have a very good chance of being successful, but might well turn the whole tide of war.

To all of this, Gates listened. He was a large, heavyset man, and one can imagine him with his chair pushed back, his waistcoat unbuttoned, his flushed face dubious yet condescendingly agreeable. Among themselves he and his associates were fond of speaking of Washington as the "great man." Now the "great man" was making an ass of himself. Afterward, Gates would tell his friends that he had given him enough rope to hang himself.

It is not too difficult, knowing the character of each man and knowing what went on between them, to re-create what was said. Gates might have taken these points one by one, ticking them off on his fingers.

Attack? My dear sir, to attack one needs an army. You don't have an army.

The Virginian would have tightened at that; there was just enough truth in it.

Your troops go always in one direction. To attack requires the other direction.

Then you have objections, the Virginian might have said. Whatever he said would be lame. He was at the disadvantage.

Many.

Would you specify them?

Gladly. Gates would have shown the "great man" no mercy.

Specific one: There are only eleven days before the enlistments run out. Your men will not attack a snowman before then. Why should they? They need only sit tight and go home.

Specific two: To attack, one needs soldiers. Your men are not soldiers.

Specific three: There is no way to cross the river and keep it from the Hessians. The crossing would take hours, and long before you ever got across, the Hessians would have their artillery on your boats. Those big Durham boats of yours make damn good targets; even a Yankee gunner couldn't miss them; and those who are not shot to pieces will drown.

Specific four: If you had twelve or eighteen thousand men instead of six thousand, you could not defeat the Hes-

sians. The Hessians are European soldiers, the best, and you
want to throw your rabble against them. Suicide.

Specific five: Your fat, foolish Boston bookseller, Mr.
Knox, has a handful of cannon left out of all the hundreds
of guns we had a year ago. A proper army wants a gun for
every fifty men. That means one hundred and twenty guns,
not twelve. The Hessians will not have to use their bayonets. They will chew you up with grape and canister before
you ever get near them.

All reports have it that Washington maintained his temper and his goodwill. He asked Gates about a night crossing, and Gates threw up his arms in despair.

Then Washington asked Gates what he, Gates, would do
in his place.

Retreat. When you cannot fight or hold a position, one
retreats.

To where?

South of the Susquehanna River. We can hold at that
river. We could build a permanent encampment there and
recruit a new army.

So much for what Gates counseled; and yet Washington contained himself and asked Gates whether, in spite of
all he had said, he would remain with the army if indeed
Washington undertook the crossing?

How could he undertake it? Gates wanted to know.

I shall, Washington said.

No. You could not.

But Washington pointed out that he was still the commander in chief, not yet Gates. What he felt inside, no one
can know, but he was apparently unruffled, calm and very
much with himself as he ushered Gates out of the Keith

house, bidding him good night as he would any honored guest at Mount Vernon.

For Washington, that night was a necessary catalyst. He made his decision. The following day, Gates and his aides rode off to Philadelphia. Washington had not relieved him of his command; he simply informed him that his little army of eight hundred men remained here in the encampment. As for Gates, he would go where he desired. He was still a brigadier; but his brigade was no longer his.

To his fellow officers, Washington said: "General Gates is ill and must go to Philadelphia and comfort himself."

[5]

IN NEW YORK CITY, a small and dedicated circle of rebels had remained in the city, lived with the memory of Nathan Hale's body swinging from the gallows and managed to keep Washington informed of most of the British movements. Now, fresh from his passage with Gates and committed to the "madness" of crossing the river, he received word from New York that Cornwallis had taken ship for England.

Washington must have breathed a long sigh of relief. Cornwallis was the only British commander he really respected, and perhaps feared too, for there was something in Cornwallis's cold and heartless determination that chilled one's blood. With Cornwallis gone back to England and the very civilized Whiggish Sir William Howe in and out of bed with the pretty Mrs. Loring, he felt that Grant would botch his command. Grant's forces were scattered all across southern Jersey.

But if Washington respected Lord Cornwallis, the British general returned the compliment and felt that there was more to the skinny, slow-speaking Virginian than most men imagined. Sitting in his cabin in the great ship of the line that would convey him back to England, Cornwallis wrote a serious letter to Colonel Rahl, the Hessian commander at Trenton:

Washington has been informed that our troops have marched into winter quarters and has been told that we are weak at Trenton and Princeton, and Lord Stirling has expressed a wish to make an attack upon those two places. I dont believe he will attempt it, but be assured that my information is undoubtedly true so I need not advise you to be on your guard against an unexpected attack at Trenton.

We do not know how reliable was Cornwallis's information as to Lord Stirling's wishes, but it is interesting to note that he respected both these men, Washington and Lord Stirling, for all of the latter's inclination to drink.

A Mr. Bazilla Haines, a Burlington County loyalist, who was engaged as an agent by the British, gave the following information, which Grant sent on to Howe in New York.

Bazilla Haines sent out to procure intelligence on the Twenty-first of December, 1776, arrived at Mount Holly in the night and lodged in the Rebel camp there. Was informed that they had only two field pieces which he thinks were three pounders as he perceived them at the church. That all the Troops were drawn up in his view, that he walked round them and he thinks that there were not above eight hundred, near one half Boys and all of them militia, a very few Pennsylvanians excepted. That he knew a great many of them, who came from Gloucester, Egg Harbor, Penns Neck and Cohansey. They were commanded by Co. Griffin.

And on the same day, the British General Grant wrote to Colonel Rahl, the Hessian commander, to reassure him that the American forces were no threat to his encampment:

Brunswick, December 21st, 1776. Sir: I have this moment received your three letters of yesterday's date. I am sorry to hear that your Brigade has been fatigued or alarmed. You may be assured that the Rebel army in Pennsylvania which has been joined by Lee's corps, Gates and Arnolds does not exceed eight thousand men who have neither shoes nor stockings, who are in fact almost naked, dying of cold, without blankets and very ill supplied with provisons.

[6]

COLONEL JOSEPH REED, Washington's good friend and secretary, was stationed down the river a day's hard ride from the Keith house. There at Bristol, he guarded the river crossing closest to Philadelphia. He had heard about the meeting between General Washington and General Gates, and though he was close to the commander, he could hardly have surmised what had been discussed. Yet he could guess that hard words had been exchanged. If anything, Reed and many others on the staff of the Virginian knew Horatio Gates better than George Washington ever did, or at least better than Washington allowed himself to know the man. Possibly because he knew and despised Gates's philosophy of retreat, Colonel Reed dispatched the following letter to General Washington:

Colonel Joseph Reed to George Washington.

Bristol, December 22, 1776.

We are all of opinion, My Dear General, that something must be attempted to revive our expiring credit, give our cause some degree of reputation, and prevent a total depreciation of the Continental money, which is coming on very fast; that even a failure cannot be more fatal than to remain in our present situation; in short, some enterprise must be undertaken in our present circumstances or we must give up the cause. In a little time the Continental army will be dissolved. The militia must be taken before their spirits and patience are exhausted; and the scattered, divided state of the enemy affords us a fair opportunity for trying what our men will do when called to an offensive attack. Will it not be possible, My Dear General, for your troops, or such part of them as can act with advantage, to make a diversion, or something more, at or about Trenton? The greater the alarm, the more likely the success will attend the attacks. If we could possess ourselves again of New Jersey, or any considerable part of it, the effects would be greater than if we had never left it.

Allow me to hope that you will consult your own good judgement and spirit, and not let the goodness of your heart subject you to the influence of men in every respect your inferiors. Something must be attempted before the sixty days expire which the commissioners have allowed; for, however many affect to despise it, it is evident that a very serious attention is paid to it, and I am confident that unless some more favorable appearance attends our arms and cause before this time, a very large number of the militia officers here will follow the example of those of Jersey and take benefit from it. I will not disguise my own sentiments, that our cause is desperate and hopeless if we do not take the opportunity of collection of troops at present to strike some stroke. Our affairs are hastening fast to ruin if we do not retrieve them by some happy event. Delay with us is now equal to a total defeat. Be not deceived, My Dear General, with small, flattering appearances; we must not suffer ourselves to be lulled into security and inaction because the enemy does not cross the river. It is but a reprieve; the execution is the more certain, for I am very clear that they can and will cross the river in spite of any opposition we can give them.

Pardon the freedom I have used. The love of my country, a wife and four children in the enemy's hands, the respect and attention I have to you, the ruin and poverty that must attend me and thousands of others will plead my excuse for so much freedom.

Your obedient and affectionate humble servant

Joseph Reed

The condition described so emotionally and urgently by Colonel Reed was specified on the same day by Samuel Brown, an American who sold information to the British, in the following report of December 22, 1776:

"General Washington's whole army does not consist of more than eight thousand men, about five thousand of them troops formerly enlisted, partly brought from Jersey by Washington and partly by Sullivan; the rest are new raised militia. That the time of enlistment of Ewing's brigade of six hundred men all expire the first of Jan. next and that the officers and men and Gen. Ewing himself have declared that they will serve no longer. That the New England troops who came with General Washington it is generally believed from their declaration that they will not serve longer than the term of their enlistment, which expires also the First of Jan'y next; that these troops compose the main part of Washington's army."

[7]

REED HAD WRITTEN HIS LETTER, and Washington had made his own commitment; yet the obstacles that faced them now were enormous. If they were to go across the river, they would have to take three or four days' supply of food with them; and the food would have to be bought. Men would have to be paid. The need for money plagued Washington as much as the British did; his pleas to Congress on that score went unanswered. And what printed paper money remained with General Mifflin had become almost worthless.

The difficulty the Americans faced in the purchase of food is reflected in this comparison of prices in British and American money. The farmers sold their produce to both, and often more eagerly to the British, who could pay with gold.

A ton of hay could be purchased by a British quartermaster from a local farmer for sixty shillings. A bushel of oats could be purchased for three shillings. It would take five hundred dollars in Continental money to buy the same amount of hay and fifty dollars to buy the oats. The British paid three shillings and sixpence for Indian corn. The Americans, using Continental dollar currency, paid twenty times as much, and for wheat, flour, bran and pork and beef, the difference was even greater.

The British made a habit of paying in gold and silver, not because British paper money was not valued by the American farmer who sold to them, but because the psychological effect of hard metal currency was so destructive to American credit—simply by the instant comparison that was forced between gold or silver and the almost worthless Continental paper. Even the Pennsylvania farmers of Bucks County, who were so much in sympathy with the American cause, went to extraordinary efforts to get their produce across the river so that they could sell it to the British for gold and silver.

Loyalty was one thing; but a little bit of hard money for hard times to come was something else entirely. Such was the speed with which the fiscal position of the Continental Congress deteriorated that everyone who looked to the future thought in terms of British hard money and had contempt for Continental dollars.

[8]

WITH THE OFFICIAL ARRIVAL of winter, the health of the army was no better. By December 22, the two military hospitals, one at Bethlehem, Pennsylvania, and the other at Newtown, Pennsylvania, were so crowded that sick and wounded men were sleeping shoulder to shoulder on the floor. The stink in these hospitals as described at the time was overwhelming, the sanitation nonexistent and the rate of death horrifying.

Taking the army as a whole, six out of every ten men were sick, and out of these six, three would never recover. Bronchitis, pneumonia and that curse of every army, dysentery, were the most common ailments; but there was also a plenitude of syphilis, gonorrhea, ulcers and liver ailments. One comes across constant mention of yellowing of the young soldiers, the skin condition that we call jaundice. Mentions of swollen bellies suggest that hepatitis was epidemic.

The army rollbooks for December 22, 1776, showed a full count of 679 officers and 10,804 enlisted men, but from this total 5,319—about half of them—were wounded, sick or on leave, leaving 6,164 fit for duty.

To reconcile figures from this period and get them to match accurately is almost impossible; also, *fit for duty* included anyone who could stand roll call. The regimental rolls were poorly kept. Desertions were so frequent that to record them accurately was impossible; and the reassignment of fragments of disintegrating companies and brigades to other commanders went on constantly.

At best Washington could order troop counts and proceed on the basis of the count on the same day as the count was taken. That he had six thousand effective men is possibly close to fact; but if he were to carry on with his plans to attack the Hessians on the other side of the river, he could by no means call upon the services of all the six thousand men. For one thing, the two hospitals had to be guarded, otherwise they could easily be overwhelmed by one of the many small detachments of British dragoons that roamed the countryside. There were precious stores to be guarded, and some sort of minimum force had to be maintained in Philadelphia to preserve civic order.

9

IT IS TO BE PRESUMED that most of that day of Sunday, December 22, was spent by General Washington in planning details of the attack he had in mind. It would be a three-pronged crossing of the river, and an enveloping attack upon both Hessian encampments, the one at Trenton and the second Hessian encampment at Bordentown under the command of Colonel von Donop.

The success of the whole project hinged on the river crossing, and that evening, as Washington pondered the problem, it began to snow. The weather had been a poor ally. It was a bitterly cold and wretched December; indeed, the presence of so much ice in the Delaware would indicate a much colder winter than we ever experience today.

As Washington worked out his plan, one thing became evident to him; either he would cross the river under the cover of darkness or the crossing would fail. If the Hessians mounted even one light cannon on the other shore, his big Durham boats could be picked off like ducks on a pond. Thus, no matter how carefully his plan was drawn, its success depended upon Colonel John Glover and his brigade of Massachusetts fishermen.

Washington sent for Glover and presented his plan for attack. One can imagine Glover, small, tight-faced and dark-eyed, sitting there opposite the tall, handsome, fair-skinned Virginian and listening to this grandiose scheme of attack, which departed casually from all realities of the army's condition at that moment. Not only that, but the mad plan was planted squarely upon the backs of the New

England fishermen. The chronic bitterness that seems to have been generated whenever General Washington faced Colonel Glover must have flowered here, and from all we can learn, Glover's initial reaction was no better than General Gates's.

The fact of the matter was that the men in Glover's brigade wanted no more of the Revolution as it was being fought. When war had been waged in New England, there had been a series of signal successes for the Massachusetts volunteers, not only in the long flight of the British from Concord to Boston, but afterward in the battle of Bunker Hill, outside of Boston.

Glover, like many New Englanders, tended to blame the present condition of the army and the present political and military disaster upon the predominance of the southern leadership. Glover's fishermen were proud, decently educated, reserved men, Congregationalists and Presbyterians: different in outlook, background, and in religion from the southerners and the Pennsylvanians.

They felt that from its very beginning they had carried the major burden of the war with no reward and no pay. Neighbors of these New England fishermen, who had remained at home and fitted out their own ships, were engaged in privateering and were in the process of becoming rich. In fact, every mail from New England brought to the fishermen in Glover's brigade news of new fortunes. There were banks in New England whose vaults were stuffed with chests of gold and silver taken from rich British ships, and, since the thin line between privateering and piracy was frequently overlooked, some of that New England money had also come from French and Spanish ships when the opportunity presented itself.

Now, sitting opposite Washington, the snow falling outside, so great a distance from his own home, his own country and his own trade, Glover pointed out to the Virginian
that he and his men had overstayed their leave. Their enlistments had expired. Furthermore, he reminded the general,
Congress, acting through the general, had promised the
fishermen two small frigates, which they could sail to their
Massachusetts home ports, and which would become the
nucleus of an American navy.

It was this promise of warships and the accompanying
hope of prize money with it that had held Glover's brigade
together. Now they were being asked to underwrite a sui-
cidal maneuver here in a strange land, in an icy river, far
from home, and to surrender any hope of the frigates, any
hope of sailing home, any hope of anything but a bloody
finish to a disastrous war.

What then could Washington have replied to Glover?
The Virginian was past promises; every promise made had
been broken, for his promises were for a congress and a
nation, and always they were ignored and rejected. Like
Glover, he had no easy way of reaching out to another man.

Yet he convinced Glover. He might have mentioned that
while Glover could return home, he, Washington could not,
and that Mount Vernon was as fair a place as Marblehead,
Massachusetts. He had never been to one, nor had Glover
been to the other. He might have told Glover that he too
hated war; but that they stood on their own soil. There was
no other justification for a man to raise a weapon against
another. Yet Nathanael Greene, who was a Quaker, would
cross the river with him. And if the odds were too great . . .

Glover might have angrily refuted any intimation that
he was afraid. He was a physically small man, and in the

presence of Washington, six feet and three inches in his bare feet, he could feel overwhelmed and very defensive. One can imagine him saying: "And did I say that I was afraid? Did I say that I would not take your lousy army across? Have I not taken them across every piece of water you came to? But I will not go down to Bristol, and I will not ferry those damned Philadelphia men. I have not enough men for that. It's a damned impossible thing to do it with your force alone, and that's all I will do and that's all that the Durham boats will do in the course of one night with the river filled with ice. And don't thank me. It's not for you that I do this but for myself and my own cause."

He would not give the fox hunter an inch, and the gulf between them remained unbridged, but likely enough Washington would have traded half his army for a few hundred men like John Glover.

Washington agreed to Glover's conditions. He knew that there were oar-propelled galleys and what were called gondolas, a sort of narrow ferry freighter, moored at Philadelphia, and he decided that somehow or other he would have these boats moved up to take the men across at the other two points. It might be supposed that in a sense he was relieved that Glover and his brigade would remain under his own command. For all of the constant estrangement and bitterness between himself and Colonel Glover, throughout the long retreat Glover's men had been the steadiest, the best disciplined and always the most dependable.

10

JOHNNY STARK of Bennington, Vermont, was one of those rare persons who are singularly blessed. Buoyant in spirit, fearless, charming, tall, long-boned, wide-shouldered, he never knew a day of ill health and he lived to be almost a hundred years old. Again and again, he risked his life, and always emerged unscathed. He was married to Molly Stark, and they could dance a night through without pause for breath. And she was wise enough to know that there were men born whom women went to like bees to honey, thus she counted her blessings and smiled instead of scowling. As for the men, they would have died for Johnny Stark, and times were that they did.

Was it any wonder that he and his Vermont boys—who were called the Bennington Rifles—were known, north to south, right through the colonies?

When Johnny Stark was twenty-four, he was taken by the Saint Francis Indians, and they held him for six weeks. He loved the life of an Indian, but he loved the girls in Bennington better; so he escaped, using his wits for a way. He had a large measure of wit. In the Battle of Saratoga, he led his men in a wild charge against a British position, and took it too, with clubbed rifles against bayonets. And they say that before he led his men into the British and Hessian guns, he called out to them:

"Yonder are the Hessians, lads. Seven pounds and ten-pence a man. What is a Bennington man worth? Tonight the flag floats from that hill or Molly Stark sleeps a widow!"

But that was still in the future when Johnny Stark and a round dozen of his Bennington boys came riding into the encampment along the Delaware. One can imagine the wild cheers as the Vermont men in their fringed shirts and leggings and fur caps came cantering down the river road, conceivably singing that wonderful song of theirs:

> Why come ye hither redcoats,
> Across the briny water?
> Why come ye hither redcoats,
> Like bullocks to the slaughter?
> Oh listen to the singing
> Of the trumpet wild and free!
> Full soon you'll hear the barking
> Of the rifle from the tree!
> Oh the rifle! Oh the rifle!
> In our hands it will prove no trifle!
> Why come ye hither redcoats,
> Your mind with madness filled?
> There's danger in our valleys,
> There's danger in our hills!

Washington welcomed him with as much delight as the enlisted men. Johnny Stark was exactly what they needed to break the spell of despair that defeat had cast over them. His first demand of Washington was not would there be an attack, but when?

They must cross the river, Washington told him.

What else are rivers for?

He talked to Glover and soothed him. They were both Yankees and they understood each other, and when he was assured by Glover that the army would be brought across, there were no doubts in his mind.

The air was electric now. The same day, Washington wrote to Colonel Reed:

General Washington to Colonel Reed.

23 December 1776.

Dear Sir: The bearer is sent down to know whether your plan was attempted last night and if not to inform you, that Christmas-day at night, one hour before day, is the time fixed upon for our attempt on Trenton. For Heaven's sake keep this to yourself, as the discovery of it may prove fatal to us, our numbers, sorry am I to say, being less than I had any conception of: but necessity, dire necessity, will, nay must, justify an attempt. Prepare, and, in concert with Griffin, attack as many of their posts as you possibly can with a prospect of success: the more we can attack at the same instant, the more confusion we shall spread and greater good will result from it. If I had not been fully convinced before of the enemy's designs, I have now ample testimony of their intentions to attack Philadelphia so soon as the ice will afford the means of conveyance.

As the Colonels of the Continental Regiments might kick up some dust about command, unless Cadwalader is considered by them in the light of a brigadier, which I wish him to be. I desired General Gates, who is unwell, and applied for Leave to go to Philadelphia, to endeavor, if his health would permit him, to call and stay two or three days at Bristol on his way. I shall not be particular: we could not ripen matters for our attack before the time mentioned in the first part of this letter; so much out of sorts and so much in want of everything are the troops under Sullivan &tc. Let me know by a careful express the plan you are to pursue.

The letter herewith sent, forward on to Philadelphia: I could wish it to be in time for the Southern post's departure, which will be I believe by eleven o'clock tomorrow.

I am, dear Sir Your most obedient servant

G. D. Washington

P.S.—I have ordered our men to be provided with three day's provision ready cooked, with which and their blankets they are to march: for if we are successful, which Heaven grant and the circumstances favor, we may push on. I shall direct every ferry and ford to be well guarded, and not a soul suffered to pass without an officer's going down with the permit. Do the same with you.

Washington's hope that General Gates might recover from his petulance and lend his advice to the amateur soldiers at Bristol was without foundation. Gates washed his hands of the whole affair and went on to plead his cause before Congress and to continue with his efforts to usurp the commander in chief and occupy the position himself.

[11]

COLONEL HENRY KNOX was commander of the Continental artillery, but actually he commanded only eighteen guns, all that were left of the hundreds of pieces of artillery that the Continentals had begun the war with. Knox was a corpulent, indulgent young man who had been a bookseller in Boston, and whose life style consisted of unshakable loyalty to and adulation of his commander in chief. His relationship to the few cannon that remained to the Continentals was like a father's relationship to his surviving children after others have perished. Knox had always proved a thorn in Glover's side; the loading and unloading of cannon every time they crossed a river, with Knox scolding and petulant, tried Glover sorely and left his men frustrated and angry.

The British dealt with an army of trained men under possibly the most severe discipline in the military world of that time; Washington, on the other hand, led an army of untrained volunteers in which perhaps thirty percent of his men were already serving past their enlistment term. In other words, he had hundreds of men in his command whose contract of service had expired and who remained with him only because of his personal persuasiveness or because of the persuasiveness of hometown officers under whom they served. The army was wracked with regional jealousies, with cliquism and with divisive bitterness between enlisted men and officers. It was Washington's task to hold the diverse elements of the army together and to turn them into a fighting force.

On the twenty-third of December, he faced the gigantic effort of organizing and mounting a counterattack with only a few days remaining before the end of the month of December and the dissolution of the army, which would follow upon the mass expiration of enlistments for the year of 1776. It is likely that well before the twenty-third, Washington had personally chosen the exact place where he would cross with his own division; and probably in his discussion with Glover, the New Englander had emphasized the fact that it would be impossible to begin the embarkation of men and cannon after dusk and take them across to the other shore in time to march on Trenton and actually strike Trenton before daylight. In order to get around this situation and be able to load during daylight, Washington chose as his point for the crossing sheltered narrows behind a tiny strip of land called Taylor Island. This island was just a few yards from the west shore of the river and grown with pines, thus shielding the west shore from observers on the east shore. With this camouflage he could begin the loading of the cannon early during the day of the attack and thus gain five or six hours for the crossing.

He had little rest during the twenty-third. Supplies, ammunition, artillery, the condition of powder and flint, the placement of the artillery and particularly the condition of the medical corps—all of these items had to be checked. Three or four officers in his army were physicians as well as soldiers, and there were also a dozen or so other doctors of varying skills who constituted the medical division. Many of these men were barbers, and their medical practice consisted of only the crudest type of surgery and was hardly something to support a full-scale battle. Washington sent messengers to the nearby towns, desperate to find additional doctors, for in one part of his mind he had to anticipate as bloody a disaster as his army had ever experienced. But out of it all, only one doctor came to him, Dr. Shippan of Bethlehem.

Another doctor, by the name of Bryant, a physician who lived on Bloomsbury Farm outside of Trenton, came seeking Colonel Rahl, who was in command of the German troops at Trenton. He was not able to find Rahl until well into the afternoon of the twenty-third, at which time he told Rahl that according to information he had from a man who had made his way across the river, rations for several days had been issued to all of the rebel army and they were planning to cross the river and attack Trenton.

"This is all nonsense! It is all women's talk," was the answer Colonel Rahl gave to him.

ON THE AFTERNOON OF MONDAY, December 23, it began to snow, and it snowed all the rest of that day and through much of the night. Under the cover of night and the snow, Commodore Thomas Seymour of Philadelphia brought the boats that would be used by the divisions under the command of General Ewing and Colonel Cadwalader up the river from Philadelphia to the two separate points of embarkation that had been chosen.

On the morning of the twenty-fourth of December, Washington came to the door of the Keith house and looked out on a snow-covered world, a silent, beautiful landscape marred only by the footsteps of the sentries and the tracks of animals. He may have reflected with some bitterness that nature appeared to have a firm alliance with the British.

After an early breakfast, he mounted and rode south along the river road to make a personal inspection of the arrangements that had been made by the two sections of his army that were under the command of Ewing and Cadwalader. This was a long, hard ride over a bad snow footing. Four Virginians of his bodyguard rode with him, and at times he was joined by General Greene, Alexander Hamilton, who was Washington's aide, and others.

During the afternoon he met with Nathanael Greene and Hugh Mercer, and they agreed that the best procedure for planning a proper attack would be to call a general staff meeting for that evening at Samuel Merrick's house, where General Greene was quartered.

In the week or so that he had been with the Merricks, Nathanael Greene had endeared himself to the family.

Thirty-four years old, Greene was a self-educated and high-ly literate blacksmith, a Quaker who had fought the inner struggle between his Quaker principles and his empathy with the rebel cause, and who in the end had turned his back on his religion and joined the rebellion.

He was a man who combined gentleness and charm with courage, a personality not unlike Washington's. The com-mander in chief valued him and cherished his friendship. Without ambition, without rancor or malice or hypocrisy, he very soon became one of the idols of the army. It was to him and Lord Stirling that Washington most frequently turned, and now Washington asked him if he could not persuade the Merricks to lend them the house that evening and to go else-where while they had a long meeting of the general staff.

The Merricks agreed to Greene's proposal, and just before dark, on the afternoon of the twenty-fourth, the offi-cers of the general staff began to converge on the Merrick home. A roll call here is interesting, and these are the offi-cers who were at the council of war, which is remembered as the "Meeting of Decision," the Merrick house being recalled as the "House of Decision," although in all truth the decision had been made already, out of necessity and desperation:

General Washington, of course, and General Greene, General Sullivan, General Mercer, Lord Stirling (that is, General William Alexander), Colonel Knox, Colonel Glover, General Adam Stephen and General Arthur St. Clair, Colonel Paul D. Sargent, Colonel John Stark and General Roche de Fermoy.

Brigadier General Arthur St. Clair was a Scotsman, who had been born in Thurso, Caithness County, Scotland, in 1734, and who had fought in the French and Indian War.

He was a difficult man, surly, quick to anger and hard put to get along with his fellow officers, a man talented in making enemies and himself his own worst enemy. Subsequently, later in the war, he was charged with treason and cowardice. There was perhaps little substance to the charges; but like Gates and Lee, he had walled himself into a reputation for ill manners and petulance.

Also present was a Lieutenant Colonel Harrison and his brother, both of them Washington's military secretaries. Fortunately, they were fussy and meticulous about their responsibility for records and correspondence. They had just finished transferring Washington's voluminous records from the Keith house headquarters to a temporary headquarters that had been set up at the little inn at the ferry terminal known as McKonkey's Tavern, which would also be used as the anchor point for the duration of the crossing.

The Reverend McWhorter was well liked by the senior officers, and for that reason and also because his judgment was well thought of, he was invited to this meeting.

[13]

UNFORTUNATELY, NO NOTES were kept of the meeting, or if notes were kept, they were destroyed for the sake of secrecy. It is quite understandable that these men, packed together in the small dining room, discussing what they proposed to do, would be far more deeply concerned with what lay ahead of them during the next few hours than with making a record of their discussion or with the judgments of history. The meal consisted of cold meat and what was called small beer, but it is doubtful that anyone thought very much of food or appetite. While the members of General Washington's staff had known to one degree or another his thinking on the subject of the crossing, only now was the final plan presented to them.

The army had been divided into three divisions. One division was under the command of Colonel John Cadwalader of Philadelphia. This included the 11th Regiment of Continental Foot, the 4th Massachusetts Regiment of Continental Foot, the 9th Rhode Island Regiment of Continental Foot, the 12th Massachusetts Regiment of Continental Foot and the Rhode Island Regiment of State Troops. The listing sounds far more impressive than it actually was, for all of these regiments put together totaled only four or five hundred men. With these, Cadwalader had under his command the Philadelphia Battalions of Associators. There were three of these Battalions of Associators and, along with them, two artillery companies, four companies of the Philadelphia City Militia and a militia company from Kent County, Delaware. Again the listing is more impressive than the numbers. The total of all troops including officers was about fifteen hundred men.

The section of the army that would cross the river at the southernmost point and attack the Hessian encampment of Colonel von Donop was under the leadership of General James Ewing. In his command was the Pennsylvania Militia Brigade, consisting of the Cumberland County Regiment, the Lancaster County Regiment, the York County Regiment, the Chester County Regiment, the Pennsylvania Militia and the New Jersey Militia, or what remained of them. Also a detachment of the 1st Regiment of Hunterdon County and of the 2nd Regiment of Middlesex County. All together they totaled about two thousand men.

The main and central body of the army, the most trusted troops, commanded by those officers whom Washington considered the most experienced in the field, would be directly under the leadership of General Washington and would make their crossing about nine miles above Trenton from behind Taylor Island.

This body of troops would consist of the following regiments, under the leadership of General William Alexander, that is, Lord Stirling: the 1st Regiment of Virginia Continental Infantry, the Regiment of Delaware Continental Infantry, the 3rd Regiment of Virginia Continental Infantry and the 1st Pennsylvania Rifle Regiment.

Brigadier General Roche de Fermoy would lead a brigade consisting of the 1st Regiment of Continental Foot Soldiers, the Pennsylvania Rifle Regiment and the Continental German Infantry Regiment. This latter regiment was raised from German farmers who at that time spoke only German and who understandably feared and hated the Hessians more than any other division of the army.

The Third Brigade under General Washington was led by General Hugh Mercer, and this included the following: the 20th Regiment of Connecticut Foot, the 1st Maryland Regiment of Continental Infantry, the 27th Regiment of Massachusetts Foot, the Connecticut State Troops and the Maryland Rifle Volunteers.

General Adam Stephen led the 4th Regiment of Virginia Foot Soldiers, Continental Infantry, the 6th Regiment of Virginia Continental Infantry and the 5th Regiment of Virginia Continental Infantry.

General Arthur St. Clair led the 5th Regiment of Continental Foot Soldiers, the 8th Regiment, which was formerly the 2nd New Hampshire Regiment, the 3rd New Hampshire Regiment and the 15th Massachusetts.

One of the largest brigades under Washington was commanded by Colonel Paul D. Sargent of Salem, Massachusetts. A quiet man, a good leader, skillful, hard-minded, we know very little about him except that he was wounded at the Battle of Bunker Hill and that after recovering from this wound he fought bravely through the rest of the war. He was a man without ambition, quietly courageous and very resolute. Under his command was the 16th Massachusetts Foot Regiment, the Connecticut Continental Infantry Regiment, the Sixth Battalion of Connecticut State Troops, the 1st Regiment of New York Continental Infantry, the 13th Regiment of Massachusetts Foot Soldiers, and the 3rd Regiment of New York Continental Infantry.

Colonel Henry Knox, the Boston bookseller, was commander of artillery for the entire army. In this case, Washington kept Knox with him—his armament consisting of eighteen field pieces. To serve and protect his guns, Knox had under his command surviving fragments of a half a dozen artillery companies. The Massachusetts Company, the New York State Company, the Eastern New Jersey Company, the Western New Jersey Company, a Pennsylvania company and a company of the Philadelphia Associators.

The final brigade was Colonel John Glover's Massachusetts fishermen. They were known as the Marblehead fishermen, because Marblehead was the hometown of Glover; but actually the brigade was gathered from a number of New England fishing towns. Of the Marblehead fishermen themselves, there were one hundred and forty enlisted men and thirty commissioned officers. Along with the Marblehead fishermen, Glover led the 3rd Regiment of Massachusetts Foot Soldiers, the 19th Connecticut Regiment, the

23rd Massachusetts Regiment and the 26th Massachusetts Regiment.

All of these groups were well populated with seamen and fishermen and were adept at the handling of boats.

In all, 2,400 men were available for the task of crossing the river with Washington. Substantial numbers had to remain behind to guard the various installations and to do other duty.

[14]

THE GENERAL PLANS for the attack were simple and direct. The three divisions of the army would cross the river together on Christmas Day by night, that is, starting the evening of the twenty-fifth of December, less than twenty-four hours after the meeting concluded. There has been a good deal written to the effect that this was done on the presumption that the Hessian troops after a day of Christmas celebration would be sodden drunk; but the actual fact of the matter is that this was as soon as the attack could possibly be mounted, and by Washington's own word, if it had been possible to mount the attack a day or a week sooner, he certainly would have done so. There has been much said about the drunkenness of the German soldiers that Christmas Day; but since only four ounces of rum per soldier was issued to them—and that soaked up by a heavy Christmas dinner—drunkenness on the part of the Hessian troops would have been a miracle indeed.

There have also been endless references to the fact that Colonel Rahl, the Hessian commander, was drunk as a "pig" at the subsequent Battle of Trenton. The truth of the matter is that he was a moderate drinker, a gentleman and a man of some compassion and breeding. His courage was never in question, and his one great weakness—which brought about his death—was an underestimation of the Continentals, whom he comprehended not at all.

Washington would lead his force across the river, nine miles above Trenton. Ewing would cross a mile below Trenton and Cadwalader would cross at the southernmost point along the river where he could attack Colonel von Donop. Every detail and facet of the attack was discussed in that meeting at the Merrick house, and all of those present who had watches synchronized them so that they might have a unified time schedule to operate with. Washington insisted that pledges of secrecy be taken.

Washington stressed the order that they must have three days of cooked food in the knapsack of every man. He was determined that if he succeeded at Trenton, he would press on from there—no more encampments now, no more retreats—and turn the war into an offensive movement by the American troops.

The smell of change and even of victory was with them that night. Much Madeira wine was consumed out of the general's own precious stores, with excitement and many toasts, and when the evening finally wound up, Washington remained awake and dictated full orders for every brigade.

It was well past midnight when the meeting at the Merrick house broke up and the officers mounted and rode off across the white snow, each to his own brigade or regiment, leaving Washington to work for hours more.

Yet, before the sun rose the following day, the events

that had taken place at the Merrick house on the twenty-fourth of December were known to the Hessians and in an overall manner the details of the coming attack were also known to them. The crossing had been betrayed before ever it took place.

[15]

WASHINGTON HAD MOVED his headquarters to the Old Ferry Inn, which was run by McKonkey and which still stands today on the west bank of the Delaware. Old McKonkey had the energy and excitement of a boy; he was heart and soul with the rebel cause, and for two days he went without sleep, cooking and serving twenty-four hours a day. He was a poor cook, but he sold his rum for Continental money and never shed a tear over it. So many of the details for crossing were worked out in his inn that he became possessive of the plan and took the position that only Washington outranked him.

Very early on the morning of December 25, General Hugh Mercer went to the Ferry House and discussed plans with those officers who were already there. This was probably immediately after sunrise, or about seven o'clock in current Eastern Standard Time, and McKonkey was already serving hot rum and milk. Mercer had expected to find Washington at the Ferry House, but Washington had returned to Mr. Keith's house, his former headquarters, in an attempt to get a few hours of sleep before the regiments began to shape up for the crossing.

Mercer heaved his arthritic body back into the saddle and rode from the Ferry House to the Keith house, where

Mrs. Keith invited him into the kitchen and gave him a cup of hot milk laced with butter and rum. Sitting there, waiting for Washington to dress in his bedroom on the floor above, Mercer told Mrs. Keith of a dream he had had the night before. In the dream he faced a large bear, but could not kill it, and bite by bite the bear savagely destroyed him. Mercer was depressed, and like so many men who have a premonition of their own death, he took no comfort from her assurances that it was only a dream. Hardly more than a week later, Mercer was killed at the Battle of Princeton.

Washington came down dressed and ready for the day to begin and willing to hear no nonsense about dreams. Mercer, who was quite depressed, told him some unwelcome news concerning the crossing. Five days before, on the twentieth of December, there had been a sudden spell of very intense cold that lasted for forty-eight hours, a cold so intense that in its upper reaches the Delaware River froze. In the thaw that followed, slabs of ice three, four and even six inches thick had broken away and were now coming down the river and in sight of the camp and the men. The upper reaches of the Delaware, where it borders Sullivan County in New York State, cut through a deep ravine. When there is a cold snap, the frost flows down into the bottom of the valley, and thus the Delaware in its high stretches freezes earlier and breaks ice more readily than almost any other river in the tidewater table of the eastern seaboard.

Now Mercer brooded moodily over the trouble the ice would make and how it would depress the men and insisted on dwelling upon the new difficulties they would have crossing the river. Washington refused to be depressed by

Mercer's lugubrious mood. Today was the twenty-fifth, and he was so excited at the prospect of the crossing that Mercer's misery had no effect upon him.

When Washington and Mercer came out of the Keith house, the Virginian's young aide, Alexander Hamilton, was waiting for him, and the party of three rode from there to McKonkey's Old Ferry Inn.

[16]

WHEN WASHINGTON GOT TO the Old Ferry Inn, Knox was working his cannon down to the river bank to be loaded onto the big Durham boats that had been drawn up in the shelter of Taylor Island. Knox was possessed of a stentorian voice, and he tended to use it too much and too quickly. His constant shouting and untempered commands had, as Washington noticed, an increasingly bad effect on the New England fishermen and on Colonel Glover, their leader. So strained was this situation that the loading of the cannon was delayed for hours, and here Washington began the task of peacemaking, a task that would continue, through angry argument after argument, for the next twenty-four hours.

Four hundred men whom Washington would lead personally in his section of the attack were already under arms and in parade, trying to appear as spiffy as four hundred freezing men, mostly in rags, might look. At ten o'clock the first lines of marching men began to move toward the Old Ferry Inn, and by noon the situation at the Ferry House was a scene of wild crowding and enormous confusion and excitement. It was the kind of excitement that exhilarates and energizes. There were no short tempers here.

Through all this, Washington was attempting to keep in constant touch with the two other divisions that were preparing for a crossing downriver. The division under the command of General Ewing was supposed to have almost two thousand men. By midday word came from Ewing that the count was perhaps five hundred less than that and that the river was full of ice. Ewing wondered whether the river could be crossed.

Washington controlled himself. Later the same day word came from Cadwalader, who was scheduled to cross below the bend of the Delaware at Bristol. Cadwalader complained that now, by actual count, he had fewer than a thousand men; and he, too, sent word back that the river was full of ice and that he did not think it could be crossed. Once again, Washington kept his temper and replied only that they were to move heaven and earth, if need be, and get across the river. It was not in his nature to understand why the simple fear of death—by drowning or any other means— should cause men to hesitate.

When he first decided to attack, Washington felt that at least the weather would be on their side; and when he awoke that morning and saw a covering of fine crisp snow on the ground, he felt confirmed in his optimism. But the frost that had begun a few days before deepened now, the sky became overcast and a wet, sleety snow began to fall, very slowly at first, but then picking up. As the day wore on into night, this snow-sleet turned into an ice-cold rain. With the sleet came a steady wind that cut through the ragged clothes of the men and drove deep into their bones, sucking out their energy.

WORKING STEADILY, INDUSTRIOUSLY and in a most disciplined fashion, Colonel Glover's men had loaded the artillery before the sun set, and in the afternoon twilight that so quickly turned into night, with the wet sleet blowing, they began the embarkation of the troops for the crossing.

The first Americans to climb into the Durham boats were the Virginian riflemen under the command of General Stephen. Washington could never overcome his bias toward Virginians in a tight situation, and of course this was noticed by the New Englanders and resented by them, particularly by the Yankees from the coastal towns.

As darkness fell, the scene around McKonkey's Inn changed from simple confusion to a kind of chaos. Dozens of men pushed to enter the inn, looking for the commander or this officer or that one. Inside the inn a blazing fire roared in the big fireplace and warmed the officers, who came in during the night, soaking wet from the rain. Washington's body servants stood by with a change of clothing for the commander in chief whenever he entered the room. But when they tried to persuade him to change, he shook them off. He drank hot rum half a dozen times during the day. It made absolutely no difference in his demeanor, and here, as in other cases, one must bow to Washington's capacity for being visibly unaffected by any amount of wine or hard liquor.

Messengers were riding to McKonkey's Inn from the whole west bank area of the river and from the two other sections of the army who were pledged to cross the river, and other riders came from Philadelphia and Baltimore. The leading citizens of the neighborhood, some of them men whose homes had been used to quarter officers, were also there, some out of curiosity, some out of a sense of the excitement and importance of the moment and still others to join the attack on Trenton.

The hundreds of men waiting for their turn to cross in the Durham boats were also around the inn, some of them crouched in the shelter of the south side, others sitting on the wet ground in their ranks, resting themselves as best they could, huddled close to each other and tightly wrapped in their cloaks.

After the eighteen cannon, which were all the artillery that the army possessed, had been brought across to the other bank, the Durham boats loaded with Virginians followed. Once the Virginians had landed, they spread out in a great half-circle and set up a chain of sentries almost arm to arm. Tory or patriot, man, woman, child, servant—anyone at all who became aware of their presence was to be made prisoner and held until such time as the crossing and the attack on Trenton had been completed.

In the course of the night perhaps thirty or forty people were taken into the sentry line and made temporary prisoners. Most of these people entered the line with no more than curiosity directing them, but at this point Washington was obsessed with the need for secrecy and would allow absolutely no loophole. Thus, local men, women and children sat in the pouring rain for hours, captive by their curiosity, many of the women and children weeping with vexation from cold and discomfort.

Until the foothold was established on the Jersey shore, Washington was tense and short with those around him, as if his desperate desire to be on both shores at once was more than he could bear. And the moment word came back that the Virginians had secured a section of the shore large enough to defend, Washington decided to cross over. Prior to this, he had felt that perhaps he should wait out the crossing and remain on the Pennsylvania shore until the last boat went over; now he could not wait.

Most Americans derive their information about this crossing from the famous painting by Emanuel Leutze, and while the children of other generations may have been inspired by the painting, in terms of a more practical approach to history it has become rather ludicrous. In the first place, by the time the crossing began night had fallen. In the second place, in the painting three men—Washington included—are standing, which would not only mark them for fools, but irritate the New England fishermen. Thirdly, the painting shows a flag that is not yet in existence. And finally, a dozen soldiers are packed into a fourteen-foot-long boat that is certainly too small for twelve men. In the background other boats are spread out across perhaps a mile of water, as if the army pushed off at a given moment, like an amphibious landing in our own time.

In actual fact, the boat Washington crossed in was between forty and fifty feet long, and it could hold forty men without crowding. It was commanded by Captain William Blackler, a Massachusetts fisherman, and in the boat with Washington were over twenty enlisted men and about a dozen officers, among them General Nathanael Greene and young Colonel Henry Knox.

The mood among the men and officers was sliding downhill. The cold, the wet snow turning to rain and the slowness with which the big Durham boats were loaded in the darkness all served to depress them. Hardly anyone was properly dressed for the weather, and the men in the boat that Washington would cross in were huddled down against the wind.

Washington stepped into the boat, picked his way among the men to where Henry Knox sat, nudged him with the toe of his boot and said vibrantly: "Shift that fat ass, Harry—but slowly, or you'll swamp the— —boat."

It dissolved the spell of despondency, and it broke up the men in the boat. As the boat pushed off, the laughter could be heard out into the river, less because of what he had said than the way he had said it. The men on the shore came to life, and everywhere, up and down the line of shivering soldiers: "What did he say?"

"Did you hear him?"

"What was it?"

In an age given to uninhibited freedom of language and a rich use of four-letter Anglo-Saxon words, Washington had an unmatched reputation for colorful speech in a crisis. What was not heard was invented, and Washington's observation gained in color and direction until it had swept through the little army. Henry Knox's buttocks became the symbol of the moment, and in that strange way that men communicate under awful conditions, the Virginia fox hunter, the haughty, reticent aristocrat, reached and touched them as he never had with noble sentiment.

18

WASHINGTON HIMSELF was high and eager, his whole body tense with excitement and purpose. Whatever occurred now, it would not happen to a man or an army in retreat or in flight or in fear. He was taking the battle to the enemy; and under these circumstances danger and discomfort had absolutely no meaning for him.

By the time the Virginian had disembarked on the east shore, it was almost eight o'clock in the evening or perhaps a half hour after eight. As yet, only a few hundred of his men had crossed the river. He set up an uncovered, unprotected headquarters in the cold sleet of the east shore—that is, a piece of wet, muddy pasture. His servants hovered around him, but he rejected their attentions. He had no intention of being coddled or of changing into dry clothes. One of the officers suggested that they build a fire, and Washington turned on him in such anger that the suggestion was not repeated. No light, no fires except the covered ember boxes for the cannon.

Someone found a box about two feet square that had once been used as a beehive, and Washington acquiesced to this as a substitute for headquarters or shelter. His men pleaded with him to sit down and rest, and he seated himself on the old beehive.

To the younger men, Hamilton, Monroe and Washington's own distant relative, the gallant Captain William Washington, the commander in chief was an old man. He was almost forty-five years old then, and the younger men were constantly amazed at his endurance and his strength.

To Washington, a man's body was a servant from which he would brook no disobedience whatsoever.

As he watched the boats arriving, his frustration and annoyance mounted. He had hoped to get his army across the river and formed up on the bank and on the march toward Trenton by midnight. This timetable was absolutely necessary if he intended to launch his attack on Trenton under the cover of darkness. But midnight came and went and the army was not yet across. By two o'clock in the morning, Washington realized with a sinking heart that the opportunity for a night attack against Trenton had been lost and that if he went up against Trenton, he would do so in daylight or not at all. And to cap this wretched turn of events, he had no news from either Cadwalader or Ewing, who should have already crossed the river.

When at last he would proceed to march with his twenty-four hundred men toward Trenton, it would be under the assumption that fifteen hundred men under Ewing were to attack Trenton from the south, while at the same time another thousand men under Cadwalader would be across the river nine miles farther south attacking the Hessian encampment of Von Donop. Perhaps of all the things that happened on this strange night, Washington can be most grateful not for what he knew, but for what he did not know. Indeed, among other things, he did not know that the Hessian commander, Colonel Rahl, was aware of every detail of the plan to make the crossing.

19

NOW WE MUST GO BACK on the same day to about 5 P.M. and see what happened at the Hessian encampment at Trenton, where Colonel Rahl was in command.

Colonel Rahl had received news of the impending Continental attacks not only from Dr. Bryant and the British General Grant but from his own informants. Once he accepted the reality of that news, swallowed his contempt for the Americans and admitted to himself that there was a possibility that the Americans could mount an attack of size and importance, he proceeded to take certain defensive measures.

He posted guard detachments that were alert and well armed all around Trenton. He also had a sort of mobile guard that marched up and down every street of the little town.

The weather in Trenton was as cold and miserable as it was at McKonkey's Ferry, where Washington and Glover and the others were undertaking the crossing. This was Christmas Day, and the Hessians, who had looked forward to the pleasures of Christmas and to a fine celebration of Christmas, were solemn and angry at the lack of piousness on the part of the Americans and particularly aggravated at their being ordered out to duty in such foul weather.

The Christmas tradition was stronger among them than it was among the Americans, and so few were their comforts that the privilege of a day of rest on December 25 was almost unassailable. Nevertheless, they were disciplined mercenary soldiers, and they responded to the orders of their officers. Now at about five o'clock, just as dusk had fallen—and on a cloudy winter day with sleet turning into rain, this dusk would be more impenetrable than usual—the Hessian encampment was attacked.

A group of Americans, possibly no more than twenty, possibly as many as sixty or seventy, dashed out of the woods, raced toward the Hessian outposts and let loose a volley from their muskets. Their gunfire was rather ragged since their powder was wet, but it had sufficient effect to kill three Hessians and to wound three others. Coming as they did so suddenly out of the darkness, the Americans appeared to be far more formidable than they actually were. At the roar of their guns, the Hessian drummers immediately beat to arms, and those Hessians who garrisoned the outpost that received the attack stood to arms calmly and began to return the American fire.

At the first sign of a Hessian response, the Americans ran away with all the speed of which they were capable. The whole affair lasted no more than two or three minutes. First there had been silence and snow falling, then the Americans dashed out of the night, firing their muskets almost point-blank at the Hessians, then the Hessians returned fire and then the Americans ran back into the night and the falling snow.

However, the brief American attack triggered the entire Hessian encampment into alertness. The Hessian troops ran to their defensive positions, and Colonel Rahl, whose horse was waiting, leaped onto the saddle and rode to the outpost that had been attacked. There he saw the three wounded and the three dying Hessians, but no Americans. Rahl dismounted and intensively questioned soldier after soldier.

The Hessians insisted that they had driven away the

Americans with very heavy losses to the Continentals. But when Rahl ordered them into the woods to find the bodies of those they claimed to have slain, they returned empty-handed. They retreated into the contention that the Americans had carried away their dead. But this conflicted oddly with their description of the haste with which the Americans had departed, running from the Hessians as if indeed the devil were after them— and pausing to pick up nothing but their feet.

Rahl ordered the entire stretch of woods in front of the attacked outpost beaten and searched, and indeed Hessian scouts moved into the forest to a mile's distance from Trenton, searching the wet woods. But the search revealed no sign of Continentals. It was the kind of attack and subsequent flight that underscored Rahl's low opinion of the Americans as soldiers. He regretted the fact that he had lost three men, but at the same time he was absolutely delighted that the predicted crossing of Washington's army and the much touted American attack on Trenton had been so wretched in character and courage and so easily beaten off.

This flaw in Rahl's character—that is, his inability to understand the mentality of men so different from the Hessian mercenaries he led—proved his eventual undoing and led to his death. At this moment, however, he was relieved and delighted.

His junior officers gathered around him, and they argued in high spirits that since the icy rain was so intense that no soldier could keep his powder dry, would it not be realistic for them to give up any thought of standing guard for the rest of Christmas Day? Rahl responded to their argument in good humor: he declared that guard duty was over and that the troops could return to quarters and pick up their festivities, eat their feast, drink their liquor and relax fully, as though this were a safe and ordinary Christmas Day at home in Germany.

Now arises the most curious and mysterious question of the whole incident of the crossing. There is no doubt that Washington's little army was saved by this attack. One would think that since this fact was soon known to so many, the attackers would come forth to demand credit, and the people at the same time would be able to determine who made the attack. But this is not the case. To this day no one knows the identity of the band of Americans who assaulted the outpost.

A claim was made afterward by Captain Anderson of the 5th Continental Infantry that this party was an advance patrol sent out by Washington, but Washington himself denied this; and since the circumstances of the crossing are so well known, no such patrol would have existed without his knowledge. For one thing, it was not until two hours after the mysterious attack that the first boatload of Virginians landed on the east shore, and they immediately set out their sentry circle for the protection of the landing spot.

Colonel Joseph Reed, in his memoirs, *Life and Correspondence*, refers to this attack as being made by an advance party that was returning from the Jerseys to Pennsylvania. But he lets it go at that, without proof or identification. What advance party were they? Why were they in the Jerseys? Why were they returning to Pennsylvania? Why did they never contact Washington? Reed identifies no one who was a member of the party, and therefore his guess is no better than anyone else's.

From the Hessian side the following explanation is given, which is perhaps more reasonable. Johannes Engelhardt, a lieutenant of artillery, was with Colonel Rahl when Rahl was questioning various officers and trying to determine the true facts about the assault. Lieutenant Engelhardt heard a Captain von Altenbockum tell Colonel Rahl that the attack had been carried out by a few farmers who had gathered together out of their rancor against the Hessians and decided to annoy the Hessians on their own account. He also said that the British General Grant had warned him that such a party of farmers was wandering in the area between Princeton and Trenton, but that Grant was totally contemptuous of them as a threat and believed they could do no harm to anyone.

However, since Colonel Rahl refused to distinguish between American farmers and American soldiers—and in this perhaps there was more than a little truth—he clung to his decision that this was Washington's doing.

One might guess that when the attack failed so dismally, the small band of farmers, shamed by their cowardice, kept silent and went home. Because communication was so ragged and uncertain in those days, they never knew the full impact of their little attack, nor had they any particular leader who would claim credit.

At McKonkey's Ferry, the soldiers climbed off the boats onto the Jersey bank of the Delaware, calling out the watchword for the day: "Victory or death."

But as midnight came and went—and half of the army was still on the other bank of the Delaware—it would appear that the prospects of victory dwindled, while those of death increased.

20

ABRAHAN HUNT, the richest man in Trenton, was a Tory. He had a fine house on the corner of King and Second streets. In his stables, directly behind the house, he kept a carriage and four horses. He was a man of substantial local position, and on Christmas Day of 1776, he felt that his social standing was confirmed. Christmas evening he gave a party. Like most parties it revolved around a particular guest of honor, in this case Colonel Rahl, commander of the German troops in Trenton.

Mr. Hunt and even more so Mrs. Hunt were devastated by the fact that the firing at the outpost kept Rahl away from the party until the late hours of the evening. However, when he joined his fellow officers and those few Trenton Tories who were in attendance at Abraham Hunt's house shortly before midnight, he proceeded to make up for lost time; and when the clock struck twelve, ushering in that very fateful day of the twenty-sixth of December, Rahl was at ease and enjoying himself hugely.

He had already put down several bumpers of hot flip—a colonial concoction of butter and rum—and had partaken of the good food, game, turkey, venison and baked pigeon and stuffed goose and fat roast ham, the good sweet cakes and the rich American pies that were so lovingly cooked and served for his appetite and approval. He relaxed in a chair, conversed with his host and the other Americans present in broken English, proved himself to be both charming and delightful and was quite happy that now, after all, Christmas in this strange, wild land would not be so different from what it might have been at home.

At the same time, nine miles to the north of Trenton, on the Jersey shore of the Delaware River, the twenty-sixth of December began for Rahl's enemy, General George Washington. Six hours before this, when he first began to move his troops across the river, word came to General Washington that Colonel Cadwalader considered the crossing to be very difficult, if not impossible. Before leaving the Ferry House to cross the river, Washington scribbled these few cold words to Cadwalader:

". . . I am determined, as the Night is favorable, to cross the River and make the attack upon Trenton in the Morning. If you can do nothing real, at least create as great a diversion as possible."

The icy, impatient fury of the commander in chief of the American forces comes bitterly alive. He made his own crossing almost matter-of-factly, and now six hours after he had crossed the river himself, Washington was standing on the east bank, wet through to the skin, his boots sodden with the icy rain that had now replaced the sleet, unhappily contemplating the fact that a large part of his army still remained on the west bank. By midnight of December 25, it appeared that his bold scheme had turned into a disaster.

All his hopes and fine calculations had been wrong. He had not been able to anticipate the quantity of the ice in the river, and above all it was the ice that made the crossing so difficult, crashing against the Durham boats and driving them downstream. Neither had he been able to anticipate the difficulty of poling the great Durham boats upstream once they were forced off course to the south. In a larger sense he had misjudged every other detail of the crossing, and now as midnight passed, he stood amidst the ruins of his plans, his dreams and possibly his country's future.

By midnight the snow and sleet had turned into cold, driving rain, and with all the necessity for the army to see, the night had become as dark as hell itself. Washington stood on the overturned beehive and directed the formation of the brigades on the Jersey side. Whatever anyone else might feel, he was so totally committed that even if all the rest of his army failed him, he alone on his chestnut-sorrel horse, a tall, skinny Don Quixote, sword drawn, war cry thrown at the dark sky, would have stormed down on Trenton, if need be, and fought his battle alone.

Several times that evening, Glover came to him and asked whether he wanted to change his plans or cancel the rest of the crossing. His response was a silent grimace to the negative. Let the army cross, there was no change in plans. Seeing him thus, the men did not question him, indeed no officer dared do so. The crossing continued, and by a half hour after two o'clock in the morning of December 26, the entire army of twenty-four hundred men and eighteen cannon and perhaps two hundred horses had been moved over from the west to the east bank of the Delaware.

If Washington had tragically miscalculated the time it would take to load the men, cannon, gun carriages, baggage carts, horses and supplies, and again to unload them in the darkness across the river, he had nevertheless accomplished a task that seemed impossible. And in a sense, the whole army was aware of the incredible achievement that night, as if indeed each soldier was threaded onto the commander's nervous system and thereby connected to his implacable determination.

21

IT WAS THREE O'CLOCK in the morning, and in three hours more, it would be dawn. There was no possibility now of a surprise attack upon the Hessians at night in the darkness or even in the early morning hours while the entire Hessian encampment slept. But for Washington the issue was already decided. They would march and they would attack.

He was not alone in his determination to move south. With him and of his mind were his beloved friend Hugh Mercer, General Sullivan, General Nathanael Greene and that rock of a man upon whom he leaned so often, William Alexander, Lord Stirling, and, of course, Johnny Stark of Vermont.

Colonel Stark was hopping with excitement and purpose. Already, the evening before, during the Meeting of Decision, he had denounced the use of troops to dig ditches and wield pickaxes. Soldiers, Stark had said, were for fighting, and now he turned to the commander in chief and demanded to know how soon they marched. Hugh Mercer, wracked with rheumatism and arthritis, living with his own conviction of impending death, joined his question to Stark's, and Sullivan, too, demanded that they march. At that moment Glover himself, perhaps because he would prefer to die rather than face the river again that night, echoed the suggestion to move south.

Glover's son John, Alexander Hamilton, James Monroe, Winthrop Sargent, young William Washington and a dozen other young officers in their teens and in their twenties let out a shout of enthusiasm, a wild Indian holler. Then the troops caught the mood, and they would have walked into hell itself if the big, skinny Virginian had demanded it.

The last boat to cross carried two pieces of the artillery, which had been reserved for the rear guard, and also four horses and ninety cannonballs. The boat was overloaded and almost went down in mid-river; the good fortune of its survival gave additional heart to the troops.

During the next hour, Washington divided the army into two sections and gave his final instructions to the commanders of the section that would march along the River Road without him. He himself would lead the other half of his troops along what was then known as the Pennington Road. No more than a few miles would ever separate the divided troops. The River Road section would be under the leadership of General Sullivan, with Colonel Stark of Vermont beside him and in a sense sharing his command. Colonel Glover would be with them, leading the 14th, 3rd, 19th, 23rd and 26th Continental regiments, all of them part of what were commonly known as Glover's Marblehead fishermen. Most of Sullivan's section consisted of New Englanders, men from Connecticut, Rhode Island, Massachusetts, Vermont, New Hampshire and Maine.

By his own side Washington kept his brilliant aide, Alexander Hamilton. Three close personal friends, Greene, Stirling and Mercer, remained with his column, as did General Stephen, who led the Virginians.

At about four o'clock in the morning the march began. The first stage would be inland to the tiny hamlet of Birmingham, about three miles' distance. Birmingham was no more than a crossroad, with a handful of houses around it, but it was the point where the River Road and the Pennington Road separated. On a clear evening a night march is slow, and even lightly armed troops in good health can average no more than three miles an hour. Here, if the men marched two miles in an hour, they would be continuing a miracle, for the troops were burdened with all they owned and with three days' food as well. And as we noted before, many of them were barefoot and most of them were exhausted after the crossing, soaked to the skin and shivering with cold. They had little energy left. Weeks of hunger and bad diet and dysentery had woefully sapped their strength.

Since Washington's northern route along the Pennington Road was slightly longer than the southern route along the River Road, Sullivan was instructed to rest his troops for fifteen or twenty minutes at a place called Howland's Ferry, thereby giving Washington's column enough leeway to march into position. Once that was done, both columns were to coordinate and attack Trenton at the same time. Since immediately before the attack the columns would be only a short distance apart, no more than seven or eight hundred yards, they were to make contact with each other just before the assault. Washington specified a dirt road that led from the Pennington Road to Beatty's Ferry as a means of communicating from army to army when they were on the outskirts of Trenton.

[22]

THERE ARE INDICATIONS that at this time, between three and four o'clock in the morning, Washington's excitement disappeared and great calm replaced it. This side of the man, the stonelike stability that alternated with fury and excitement, has been observed by many who knew him and, interestingly, about a week before the crossing, Thomas Paine had written in the first *Crisis* paper:

"Voltaire has remarked that King William never appeared to full advantage but in difficulties and in action. The same remark may be made of General Washington, for the character fits him. There is a natural firmness in some minds, which cannot be unlocked by trifles; but which when unlocked, discovers a cabinet of fortitude; and I reckon it among those kinds of public blessings which we do not immediately see, that God had blessed him with uninterrupted health, and given him a mind that can flourish upon care."

An eyewitness picture of the crossing and march was later recorded by Elisha Bostwick of the 7th Connecticut Regiment:

"Our whole army was then set in motion and toward evening began to recross the Delaware, but by obstructions of ice in the river did not all get across till quite late in the evening, and all the time a constant fall of snow, with some rain, and finally our march began with the torches of our fieldpieces stuck in the exhalters. They sparkled and blazed in the storm all night, and about daylight a halt was made, at which time his Excellency and aides came near to front on the side of the path where the soldiers stood.

"I heard his Excellency as he was coming on speaking to and encouraging the soldiers. The words he spoke as he passed by where I stood and in my hearing were these:

" 'Soldiers, keep by your officers. For God's sake, keep by your officers!' "

The artillery was divided, ten pieces under the command of Knox, to go along with Washington in the northern section of the army, and eight pieces to go along with Sullivan in the southern section of the army.

The rain grew heavier, and about half past five in the morning, young Captain John Mott, who led a regiment of Jersey Continentals, found it impossible to keep the powder in the priming box of his musket dry. He ran along checking the guns of his own regiment and found that this was the case with all the muskets he touched. He then went to General Sullivan and to Colonel Johnny Stark, who were in command, and told them that as far as he could determine every gun in the division was incapable of being fired. Sullivan and Stark stopped the march and sent runners out along the column to tell each regimental leader to examine the powder pans on the muskets. After a few minutes the reports came back and they both decided that while it would be possible to fire the artillery, it would be only by a miracle that any of the muskets in the column could spark and ignite. There was no way to keep the flints dry. And such was the moisture in the air and the horizontal cut of the driving rain of what had turned into a true northeaster, that any thought of keeping the powder dry too was at this moment only a dream.

Johnny Stark insisted that they go on, and be damned with whether the guns could be fired. Stark, backed up by his handful of Vermont riflemen, had a very small opinion of muskets in any weather, and as far as he was concerned, most musket fire was all sound and fury. He had heard the story of what happened to the Virginia and Carolina riflemen in Brooklyn. But they were not his Bennington boys, and he said to Sullivan that he would think a damn sight more of a Continental lad with an unloaded musket and a bayonet than of one with a loaded musket and no bayonet.

As for his own lads, they would swing their rifles like clubs, and if they broke their rifles, they'd break a Hessian head or two with them.

Sullivan, however, could not accept the fact that soldiers were planning to attack a strong and disciplined garrison without any firepower, and he told Captain Mott, one of his aides, to ride north across the fields to the Pennington Road and intercept the other column and ask General Washington for orders.

Going across the icy fields in the blackness of that night was no small feat, yet Mott found Washington, summed up the situation briefly and asked Washington for orders.

At that moment, Washington's controlled calm collapsed and he roared that Sullivan had his damned orders. Then he stared at the shriveled Mott for a moment and added, more calmly, "Tell him to advance and charge!"

When Mott rejoined Sullivan, Stark and Glover and repeated precisely what the commander had said, it had the same effect upon the men as Washington's observation in the Durham boat on the width of Knox's backside. It was greeted by the soaked, freezing officers with a burst of laughter, and then the language of Washington, and the laughter raced up and down the line, once again bringing the men to life.

[23]

SOLDIERS, MARCHING BY NIGHT in ranks, can and do fall asleep on their feet without halting their march until they come to some obstacle that tumbles them. This happened to both columns of the attacking army. At first they marched on their feet through the freezing rain, dozing for the first two or three miles. Then they began to stumble and fall with increasing frequency.

They would fall into the slush and cold mud and lie there sleeping, and the officers would spur back and forth, shouting, kicking the men awake, pleading with them. Washington himself rode up and down the column constantly, calling to the men, begging them to keep their eyes open.

There were no surfaced roads in America in those days, except for small paved stretches in the cities. Ordinary traffic under a rain would turn the rutted surface of the dirt roads into slippery mud, and the passage of so many men as this would create a muddy slough six or seven inches deep. Again and again, the men fell and the horses slipped, and sometimes crippled themselves. Not only was the confusion almost beyond repair, but the men—and of this they were supremely unaware—were being transformed into perhaps the most threatening-looking body of men that had ever constituted an army.

Their arms, legs and faces were caked with mud. Their long hair was tangled, filthy, and the clothes of most of them were in tatters.

[24]

THE BATTLE OF TRENTON began a few minutes before eight o'clock in the morning, on the day after Christmas, 1776. At that time, the column led by Washington, Stirling, Mercer and Greene paused at the edge of Trenton. The village was now visible, misty in the rain.

Captain Thomas Forrest was at the head of the column, with two light fieldpieces. Forrest was a Philadelphia youngster with a passion for artillery, and he commanded two of Knox's precious cannon. Now Forrest was approached by a local farmer, who had come out early to replenish his woodpile. The farmer was surprised but not frightened by the materialization of this incredible-looking army out of the morning mist.

"Where are the Hessian pickets?" Forrest asked him.

Now the other officers had ridden up and dismounted, and the farmer found himself the center of attention, with fine, if wet, gentlemen listening to every word he said. He knew the preciousness of the moment that had hanged him on a peg of destiny, and afterward he stated that he had spoken directly to Washington, whom he knew because he was a good head taller than anyone else.

The farmer pointed out a Hessian sentry, a small blur of a man through the rain. "He's asleep," the farmer said with contempt. "I walked by his nose and he never saw me." The house right behind him contained the Hessian outguard, eight to twelve men, but they, too, were likely enough sound asleep. There had been trouble the day before. The Hessians were up late and they would sleep late.

Young Captain William Washington and young Lieutenant James Monroe—later to be President of the United States—sat on their horses on either side of the older Washington. They were delightful and courageous young men, who lived their war experience with style and bravado. Captain William Washington was twenty-four years old at that time and had already made himself an unmatched reputation for courage and daring. William Washington served under Hugh Mercer, whom he adored, and who regarded him much as an adopted son. In the Battle of Brooklyn, Captain Washington acted with outstanding bravery, and he was severely wounded. Still not recovered from his wounds, he made the retreat through the Jerseys with the army, never lagging or complaining. Now he stood tight in his stirrups, trembling with eagerness and excitement.

Washington pointed to the sentry at the house and indicated that it would be very much to their advantage if they could cut down the sentry, isolate the house and silence the guard detail inside it.

Certainly Washington never meant this to be done by two men. But without waiting for reinforcements or for any additional instructions, William Washington and James Monroe spurred away. They drew their sabers, cut down the sentry before he was properly awake and then flung themselves off their horses, smashed into the house and began the Battle of Trenton.

This house belonged to the Howell family of Trenton, coopers or boxmakers by trade. It was one of several dwellings that the Germans, according to their military customs, had selected as outposts, or guardhouses, during the time of their encampment at Trenton. The guards occupied the ground floor of the building and in the Hessian custom had stacked their arms at the door behind the sentry. When William Washington and James Monroe cut down the sentry and raced to the house, the two young men were at the same time able to ride their horses over the stacked arms, smashing and scattering the muskets, and by so doing deny the arms to the men inside. There were nine German sol-

diers in the house, and subsequently at court-martial proceedings they claimed that they had driven off the Americans. But the plain fact of the matter was that the Hessians,
deprived of their arms, tumbled through the rear windows,
surrendering the house thereby, and ran like the very devil
toward Trenton.

In this precipitous retreat, the Hessians were sent on
their way by their lieutenant, who kept yelling at the top
of his lungs:

"Der Feind! Der Feind! Heraus! Heraus!"

"The enemy! The enemy! Out! Out!"

When General Washington saw the two boys sweep
down upon the guardhouse alone, he spurred his horse
around to face his troops, shouting at the top of his lungs:
"Forward! Damn you—attack!"

Captain Forrest swept ahead with his two light guns, the
men running behind him. Knox was cut off for a moment
with his larger battery of six cannon, and Washington
yelled at him to get his guns up front where they could
assault the enemy, since the muskets were finished as
firearms in the pouring rain. Young Alexander Hamilton, at
a look from the commander in chief, spurred back to help
Knox clear a path for his guns and bring them up. Mercer
rode up shoulder to shoulder with Washington, and the two
of them cantered in front of the running men, the vanguard
of the whole column of twelve or thirteen hundred men that
were pouring toward Trenton. (Sullivan's column on the
River Road was still separated from them.)

And that was the moment when William Washington
and James Monroe cut down the sentry and scattered the
muskets of the Hessians.

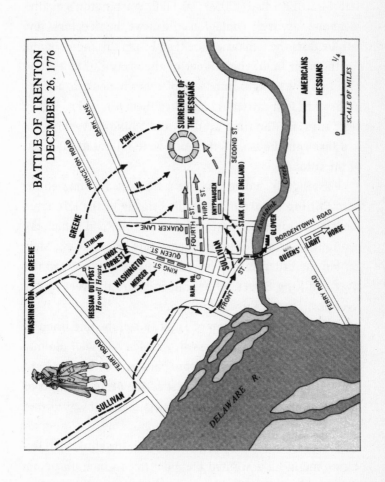

BATTLE OF TRENTON
DECEMBER 26, 1776

AMERICANS
HESSIANS

SCALE OF MILES
0   ¼

SURRENDER OF THE HESSIANS

PENN.

VA.

DARK LANE

PRINCETON ROAD

GREENE

STIRLING

WASHINGTON AND GREENE

HESSIAN OUTPOST
Howell House

KNOX
FORREST

WASHINGTON

MERCER

RAHL HQ.

FERRY ROAD

SULLIVAN

QUAKER LANE

QUEEN ST.

KING ST.

FOURTH ST.

THIRD ST.

FRONT ST.

KNYPHAUSEN

SULLIVAN

STARK (NEW ENGLAND)

SECOND ST.

Assunpink Creek

GLOVER

BORDENTOWN ROAD

QUEENS'

LIGHT HORSE

FERRY ROAD

DELAWARE R.

25

THE SOLDIERS HAD COME TO LIFE. Washington's excitement and fury were contagious. He drove the sleepiness and fatigue from the exhausted men; and from this moment and for the next hour, the temper of the army tightened and rose to a fever pitch. Hundreds of eager hands grasped the mud-caked gun carriages and rolled them forward as if they were toys. By the time Monroe and William Washington had taken the house, all the guns were rolling at the front of the column.

Washington's voice was like a trumpet. He shouted for Lord Stirling to take off with his brigade to the left, from the Pennington Road toward the Princeton Road, which lay just to the north of Trenton. Meanwhile he and Hugh Mercer led the other part of his column sideward toward the river and King Street, which ran from Front Street by the river north to the Princeton Road.

The Philadelphia Troop of Light Horse, the one troop in the army that was well dressed, well fed and well mounted, swarmed around Washington. Thus as the morning light increased, they made for the rest of the army the kind of handsome and encouraging military parade that was so rare in the American experience.

Now a storm of cheering burst forth, for all that Washington might have wanted the quiet to continue. But guns had been fired, the silence had been shattered and the Hessians by now knew that they had been attacked. The cheering increased until the entire command under Washington were screaming at the top of their lungs with wild excitement and exultation.

Washington's shouts of "Forward!" were lost in the noise. He led them on, officers and men racing with all their speed toward the village.

One must see this sight as the Hessians saw it moments later. Most of the twelve or thirteen hundred men were half-naked. All of them were soaking wet and covered with mud. Most were barefoot, their hair so long that frequently it came down below their shoulders, their faces covered with scrubby beards, yelling, cursing, waving their wet bayonet-carrying muskets, appearing magically and mysteriously out of the rain and mist and pouring down upon the sleepy and unprepared garrison of Trenton. Perhaps in the entire American Revolution, no wilder, no more chaotic scene than this had ever taken place.

It also had its comic-tragic-mad aspect. From the very beginning of the movement toward Trenton, everything had gone wrong. And here at the end of the road to Trenton things continued to go wrong; yet, in this, too, there was a kind of insane logic, as if fate had stacked a series of lunatic events to add up to some kind of inverted sanity at the final moment.

At the same time that General Washington had ordered Lord Stirling and General Greene to the left and Hugh Mercer to the right, General Sullivan's army was marching down the River Road where it bends toward the river and Front Street in Trenton. About six hundred and fifty or seven hundred yards separated them from the place where William Washington and James Monroe had driven the Hessians out of the guard-house. Sullivan could hear the shouting of men in the distance and the snapping of the few Hessian guns that were fired, and then they heard the sound of Knox's cannon. By now all of Trenton was awake and in an uproar.

Johnny Stark, who was with the rear guard on the River Road, spurred his horse up the column past a regiment of New Hampshire men and yelled with all his voice for the New Englanders to follow him. In this column, Colonel Stark was subordinate in command to General Sullivan, to General St. Clair and even to Colonel John Glover, but all of this mattered not at all. Here was a battle beginning, in hearing but out of sight, and Johnny Stark of Vermont realized that it might be over before he reached it. So he yelled for all Vermont and New Hampshire men to follow him and to get to hell into the fighting, because that was where they properly belonged, or did they want the whole damned world to belong to Virginia?

However much Sullivan might have resented Stark's taking command of the attack—Stark, an outsider, not even a brigadier, a wild man from the Green Mountains who had ridden down because he could not bear for anything important to take place without his presence—however much he might resent this, Sullivan had enough sense to know that battles were won by precisely the kind of verve men like Stark could generate. In any case, the movement was under way; to try to stop it would have meant a disaster, and a moment later the pace of events became too fast properly to record, much less halt.

Yelling like a madman, Stark led the way, and matching his screaming Indian shouts, the New Englanders poured after him. More than the first gunfire, this blood-curdling sound awakened the Hessians from their sleep.

26

THE HESSIAN TROOPS poured out of their quarters and formed up on Third and on King streets. Their muskets were loaded, and they were able to get off a volley of heavy musket fire against the Americans. But their brains were addled, their minds were heavy with sleep and their musketry was woefully inaccurate. No Americans were hit on this occasion or anywhere else during the battle, only William Washington and James Monroe in their first swoop on the guardhouse. It must be remembered that the wide-bore musket of the time was an extremely inaccurate weapon, except at close range. It must also be remembered that memories of this battle were as confused as the battle itself, and perhaps most of the Hessian muskets missed fire. We know at least a handful of the Virginia and Pennsylvania riflemen were able to fire their weapons, but we cannot be certain that many Hessian muskets were actually discharged in the rain, even though the reports from both sides say they were.

The Hessians on Third Street were pointing their muskets toward Johnny Stark and his New Englanders. But since their firing was inaccurate, if indeed their powder ignited at all, no one was hit. Sullivan turned his own attention to his field guns, the eight pieces of cannon that had been allotted to him. He faced the same difficulty Knox had in moving the guns to the front of the suddenly sprinting column. But now his force, too, had caught the excitement of battle and joined their wild shouts to those of Washington's army, although about three hundred and fifty yards still separated the two columns, with the village of

Trenton between them. Sullivan's men broke ranks to handle the big guns. By the time Washington and Mercer had started their advance toward King Street, Sullivan's cannon were cleared for action and firing point-blank into the Hessians.

It was now a few minutes after eight o'clock, and all three columns—three of them now since Washington had divided his division into two columns—were pouring into Trenton. Colonel Johnny Stark led the New Englanders, and Sullivan and St. Clair led the rest of the River Road column. Washington and Mercer led part of Washington's column, and Greene and Lord Stirling led the other part. The town now resounded with a crazy cacophony of sound, the Hessian drums beating to arms and twenty-four hundred Americans yelling with excitement.

The troop of the Queen's Own Light Horse who were quartered in Trenton with the Hessians behaved badly indeed. It would seem that from the very moment the battle began, the dragoons panicked completely. They were trained cavalry-men from one of the best British horse regiments. Now they had only one thought in mind, to saddle their horses and get out of Trenton.

Some of them managed to saddle up. Others mounted bareback. They rode here and there through the town, staying together until they found an escape route down Fourth Street to the right along Quaker Lane and then down Second Street and out of Trenton.

Where the bewildered Hessian soldiers stood in their way, the British dragoons galloped right over them. Some of the Hessians shouted at them with fury, and other Hessians waved their guns at the dragoons; but their muskets were wet and impotent.

If these British dragoons, who were mounted on large, fresh and well-trained horses, had rallied and kept their nerve, they could have cut back and forth through the American army like a scythe cuts dry grass. The Americans were laced with fatigue and at their last limits of strength— and even a small diversion by the dragoons might have turned the tide and made Trenton a bloody defeat for the Continental army.

The Hessians had been too suddenly awakened. They rushed to the windows of the houses where they were quartered; they smashed the glass with their musket butts and fired blindly into the street. But most of them had neither the heart nor the coordination to reload. Those who came out into the rain allowed their firing pans to get wet. As with the Continental muskets, once fired, the Hessian muskets were also worthless as firearms.

Pouring out of the houses where they were quartered, the Hessians were too disciplined to act as individuals. If they had gone into the defensive immediately, if they had simply fixed their bayonets and rushed at the Continental soldiers who were now swarming through the streets, they might have turned the attack into a rout for the Americans. However, their first action was not to stop the Americans but to form their ranks in the streets. This attempt at discipline with enemy seemingly everywhere failed dismally.

[27]

TRUSTING GLOVER'S FISHERMEN more than any others of the troops he led, Sullivan had asked the New Englander to take command of the cannon and to use them according to his own judgment once the battle began. Queen Street in

Trenton ran directly through the center of the town from north to south and on the southern end crossed over the Assanpink Creek on a small bridge. As Sullivan's men drove down Front Street, Glover saw the bridge and decided that, above all, his cannon must get there, thereby bottling up the Hessians by closing their main escape path.

At this point, about half past eight in the morning, it would seem that out of a common wild enthusiasm generated by their exhilaration, the Americans had decided that there was no question anymore as to who had won the Battle of Trenton. Also, since they were apparently invulnerable, and since no matter how many Hessian guns were pointed at them, no one was hit—the Hessians were already running down Queen Street to make their escape from the town—there was the objective proof that the day was theirs.

Glover acted on this assumption of victory and ran his guns across the little bridge, occupying the high ground south of the bridge, closing off the road across Assanpink Creek. But only after the last of the British dragoons had fled from Trenton.

There were stationed in Trenton then a small troop of Hessian chasseurs who evidently were infected with whatever disease took hold of cavalrymen that day. Like the British, they leaped onto their horses with no other thought than to get out of town. These horsemen, too, were able to evade Glover's trap by turning left to Second Street and riding out of town on the north shore of the creek. Almost a hundred Hessian foot soldiers ran after them and made good their escape.

By now Sullivan's New Englanders had driven across the southern part of the village and along with Glover's men and the artillery regiment closed it off as an avenue of retreat.

When Washington's men exploded with their screaming shouts and ran to attack Trenton, the Virginian realized that the one function of gunpowder remaining to him,
his ten pieces of artillery, would be outdistanced by the
running men. Therefore, he had spurred his horse back and
forth across the front of his troops, shouting and pleading
with them to slow down and not outrun the cannon.

"Stay in place and follow your officers," he begged them.

The officers caught his intention and slowed the march,
and then Washington shouted for Captain Forrest to keep the
brace of guns that were under his command always in front
of the men. The remaining guns, now under the command of
Knox, moved off to the left with the two brigades that were
under the command of Lord Stirling and General Greene.

Washington continued to rein his big horse, giving
directions to his staff, calling upon the officers by name to
hold back the excited troops and to keep them in order, so
that they might answer as a disciplined force to a call for
action. This was hardly as simple as it sounds, for the battle was raging toward its climax.

Meanwhile, down along King Street toward Colonel
Rahl's headquarters, the Hessians were lining up and getting into regimental rank. They had wheeled three of their
bright shining brass pieces of artillery into firing position;
and when Captain Forrest saw this, and without checking
his aim too carefully, he let go at the Hessians with his
whole battery. The guns were loaded with canister and,
though not too well aimed, they nevertheless killed three
of the horses that were being used by the Germans to wheel
the brass fieldpieces into position and two of the artillery-
men as well. For the moment Forrest's cannonade toppled
the guns and put the Hessian artillery out of action.

Washington shouted to Forrest to aim his guns properly. Alexander Hamilton came riding up alongside of the general, yelling to be heard in his piping voice, shrilled into a falsetto, telling Washington to take cover and not to expose himself. Mercer, who was some fifty feet ahead of Washington, echoed the warning. Washington shook his head angrily. Always a brilliant and flashy horseman, he reined his horse around, causing it to prance on two legs, and then whipped it toward the Hessians.

The Americans could no longer be held in check, and screaming like maniacs, they broke ranks and swarmed down upon the German artillery and upon the space in front of Rahl's headquarters, where the Hessians had managed to get themselves into a sort of parade line.

By now there were perhaps three or four hundred Hessians in position, but when they saw pouring down upon them the mud-covered madmen that the Americans had become, hair flying in the wind, bayonets thirsting for action, the Hessians lost their nerve and fled. This was the first time in the course of the Revolution that a Hessian regiment had ever broken under attack.

Now Colonel Stark caught a clear view of Washington on his horse, looming up over the fleeing Hessians. Stark let out a wild shout that was echoed by the New Englanders behind him. At full pace they drove into the retreating Hessians, bayonetting and literally knocking them over by sheer body contact, plowing down the field and clearing all opposition out of their way.

Afterward the Germans, with their passion for order and discipline, tried to make a pattern out of this wild, gunpowderless battle that had no pattern at all. For one thing, they insisted to the very end that Washington had stormed into the town with six thousand men. By saying this they were not excusing their own defeat but were simply trying to understand how they had been overwhelmed so quickly and so completely.

[28]

RAHL, THE HESSIAN COLONEL, was roused out of his bed after the screaming Continentals had poured into the outskirts of the little town. He pulled on his clothes but would not leave his room until his military jacket was at least partly buttoned. Even facing imminent disaster, he could not overcome his long training and leap naked to the defense of the encampment.

He ran out of the front door of the house, mounted his horse and rode back and forth on the street calling in a loud, steady voice for his men to be calm and to remember that they were Hessian soldiers.

At this point the Americans were less than fifty yards from where Rahl rallied his men and coming on very fast. It can be said to Rahl's credit that he was without fear, calm and collected. Never for a moment did he panic or lose his head. He shouted to his men to follow him, which they did in good order. Wheeling his horse and holding it to a tight trot, he managed to lead several hundred of his men down Third Street and to the left to Fourth Street, up on Quaker Lane and then off Quaker Lane into a pasture. Once in this pasture, he reined his horse around and called to his men to form up and make a defensive square.

The Hessians rallied to Rahl's control and military posture. They ran toward him from every direction. Rahl ordered them to form a three-sided square facing the Americans, who now were leaping over fences, racing through backyards, as well as along Third Street and Fourth Street and down from the Princeton Road through the north end of the town toward the pasture.

Catching sight of Colonel Rahl sitting on his horse in the pasture, so calm and rocklike, issuing his orders as if he were on a parade ground, several of the mounted Hessian officers rode through the Americans to be at his side.

It must be remembered that except for a few rifles in the hands of soldiers who had kept their primer dry in closed powder pans and who had been told to hold their fire for Hessian officers, the American small arms were wet and useless. Unless the Americans could bayonet the Hessian officer as he rode by, there was nothing they could really do to impede his progress. They might try to grab at his reins and pull up his horse, but a Hessian officer would be cutting left and right with his saber. Half a dozen Hessian officers on horseback managed to gather around Rahl, demanding that he order a retreat.

What we know of this conversation between Rahl and his staff comes at third and fourth hand from those soldiers in Washington's army who came out of the German population in Pennsylvania and who thought at least they could understand and remember what the Hessian officers had said. It would seem that Rahl kept shouting at his officers to be calm and to tell him how many Americans were in Trenton.

The phrase in German: "How many are there?" seems to have been repeated over and over.

No one knew, and no one could guess. The answers ranged from four thousand to six thousand men.

The insistence on retreat angered Rahl, and for the first time he lost his composure and shouted at his fellow officers to end this talk of flight. He called to his Hessians to fix bayonets and prepare to attack. A trumpeter joined them and managed to sound a Hessian bugle call. Several drummers came running across the pasture, beating to arms as they ran. In a matter of minutes Rahl had turned a disorganized, retreating, frightened group of men into a disciplined little army that was ready to fight.

Rahl looked at them with pride and pleasure, shouted his own war cry, drew his sword and gave the order to advance. He spurred his horse in front of them and then checked it, so that it pranced properly, like a well-trained horse at a cavalry display.

The mood of the Hessians had changed completely now, and Major Knyphausen rode after Rahl, echoing his shouts to attack. At that moment one of the Pennsylvania riflemen who had kept his powder dry, one of no more than a handful among the Continental forces, drew a bead on Rahl and shot him.

Rahl swayed in the saddle, dropped his sword and cried out that he was hit. Now the Hessians ceased their advance and they turned toward Rahl, looking at him desperately and waiting for him to lead them again. Rahl said again that he was wounded, and Major Knyphausen attempted to ride out in front of him and take his command. Knyphausen sat there on his horse, waving his sword for the Hessians to follow him, but the wounding of Rahl had broken the spell that the gallant colonel had woven.

For perhaps thirty seconds the Hessian soldiers remained in a tight group around their wounded commander. Then they broke, most of them throwing down their useless muskets, and ran across the fields to the south in the direction of Assanpink Creek.

The shot that wounded Rahl had probably come from a member of Colonel Hand's brigade of Pennsylvania riflemen. The riflemen, running swiftly at the head of the advancing American forces, had poured north across the meadow from the junction of Fourth Street and Quaker Lane. Washington spurred after them, Colonel Hand at his side, shouting for the Pennsylvanians to form up in a long line and block any retreat to the north.

For the moment, this maneuver was successful, and then perhaps a minute later General Greene's men came running down from the direction of Dark Lane to back up the Pennsylvania riflemen and spread the net still further.

One must remember that all of this happened more quickly than the telling. No more than two or three minutes passed between Rahl's rallying his men and his being wounded. During that time Washington was riding toward this center of action.

In the course of this action, Washington's horse was shot under him. Nobody appeared to remember exactly when it had happened, but everyone agreed that Washington's response had been one of irritation as he leaped clear of the falling animal. At his age, almost forty-five, he was remarkably agile. He had gone two nights without sleep. Considering how many times he had paced the column in two directions, back and forth, he had ridden at least thirty miles since crossing the river. Again and again he had dismounted, leading his horse by hand and talking to the men, whispering to them, consoling them, begging them to overcome their fatigue and to hang on. In spite of this, he was out of the saddle of the dying horse and swinging up onto a new mount almost in a matter of seconds. Like his men, he had transcended himself and was lost in the excitement of the battle.

Apparently his second horse was a white, and this was characteristic of the legend that had already grown up about him and his white horses. The Virginians, who were perhaps two hundred yards to the north of where Washington lost his mount, could see the horse with the man on it. They sent up a yell of anger and poured down the pasture to support their commander in chief. At the very same time, Johnny Stark and his Vermont and New Hampshire men were racing up from the south. Suddenly the force of Hessians—there were almost eight hundred of them that Rahl had rallied into action—found themselves inside a circle of Americans.

Rahl continued to sit on his horse, losing blood and heartbroken at what had happened. The defeated Hessians stood where they were. They presented their wet muskets almost as objects of atonement.

Washington misunderstood their gesture of surrender and imagined that they were forming up to fire a volley into the Americans. Afterward, some people censured him for this. But it is impossible to conceive that in the excitement of the moment he would have remembered or even taken the chance that no musket could be fired on that day in that weather. In any case, Washington shouted for Captain Forrest to fire into the Hessians, and if this order had been obeyed, a storm of canisters would have torn through their close-packed ranks and perhaps hundreds of them would have been cruelly cut down. Fortunately, young Captain Forrest kept his head, and he ran up to where Washington sat on his horse and shouted to him: "Sir, they have struck!"

Washington leaned over his horse now and looked down at Forrest's smoke-blackened face.

"Struck?" Washington asked.

"Yes, sir, their colors are down!" Forrest yelled.

The exchange with Forrest appeared to bring Washington to his senses. Suddenly the fury left him and he became very cold and formal. He rode his horse toward the Hessians, Captain Forrest and Captain Hamilton pressing after him, and after them the shouting mob of American soldiers. As the great mass of bearded and unkempt Americans, their rags hanging from wet and mud-grimed bodies, pressed around the cluster of Hessians, they saw now the fear that had gathered over the Hessians' faces. Now the Hessians were no longer the hated and frightful enemy. They were German boys, very far from home, facing a mob of wild men, who already were so close with their naked bayonets that the Hessians believed that their last moment on earth had come.

All the hunger, all the terrible defeats that the Americans had experienced over the past six months were summed up in their anger now; yet, when they saw the pale dread, the horror on the Hessians' faces, the Americans stopped.

[29]

MEANWHILE SULLIVAN'S MEN had closed around Rahl and Knyphausen, who was holding Rahl erect in his saddle. On the other side of Rahl, also on horseback, was a young Hessian officer, who with Knyphausen was supporting his commander.

Rahl dropped his sword, and a Hessian soldier picked it

up and gave it to him. His hands trembling, tears running down his cheeks, Rahl reversed his sword and said in German that he must surrender like a Hessian officer.

Hundreds of Americans pressed around the three mounted Hessian officers, staring up at them curiously. The great battle shout became a whisper, and the whisper gave way to the sound of the rain, and suddenly a stillness settled over Trenton.

Sullivan called to his men to find someone who spoke German, and a young German captain from Pennsylvania pushed through the mass of Americans to face Rahl.

Washington, however, kept his distance, observing the scene from about thirty yards away. He made no attempt to get through the intervening space and join Sullivan's confrontation of Rahl. The young Pennsylvania captain translated for Sullivan, telling Sullivan that Rahl wanted to surrender like a Hessian officer. Sullivan replied with words to the effect that he didn't give a goddamn how Rahl surrendered, so long as he surrendered. He reached out and took the sword, looked at it for a long moment and then passed it over to Johnny Stark.

Knyphausen then talked to Sullivan in German, and the young Pennsylvania officer translated for him, saying that now he, Knyphausen, was in command, since it appeared that Colonel Rahl was hurt very badly, and that he, too, would surrender.

Then Knyphausen drew his sword, reversed it and gave it to Sullivan.

He then asked Sullivan would it be all right if they found a place where Rahl could lie down and where his wounds could be attended to? When this was translated for Sullivan, the American said yes, and he ordered off a guard to accompany them. Slowly, the three Hessian officers on their horses moved through the crowd of Americans.

Sullivan then pushed his way through the Pennsylvanians to where Washington sat with his staff officers and aides. Old Hugh Mercer was at his side. Mercer was suffering great arthritic pain. But he was so exhilarated with what had happened that he was able to ignore the pain and participate in the triumph over the Hessians.

From the expression on Washington's face it was evident that this was no triumph for him. The forty-eight hours that he had just lived through caught up with him, and his body sagged with fatigue. Sullivan reported to him, and then Colonel Stark pushed through and talked to him, and then other officers, one after another. The officers who had pressed around Washington now went off to the business of concluding the victory and gathering their men.

Meanwhile, the guard of a dozen men that Sullivan had detailed to go with the Hessian officers accompanied Rahl, Knyphausen and the young officer to the home of Stacey Potts. Potts was a Quaker and a tavernkeeper, and like most of the Quakers in Trenton, he had remained in the town after its occupation by the Hessians. The Quakers in Trenton had carried themselves in a remarkable manner throughout this battle. They had remained in their homes without panic and without excitement, and throughout the fighting they had administered to the wounded of both sides. They had bound the wounds Captain William Washington had suffered in the initial attack on the guardhouse, and they had bound up the wounds of the Hessians.

The two Hessian officers, assisted by two more Hessian enlisted men, carried Rahl into the Potts home and upstairs to the second floor. Potts told them to lay the colonel down on a bed in the front room, that is, on his own bed. Potts's daughter had suffered a slight skull wound, and her head was bound up. Pale, quiet, she watched the whole thing, and only when Rahl had been laid out on the bed did she come toward him and help her mother to cut away his blood-soaked clothes and to see whether or not they could attend to his wound.

As unbelievable as it sounds, only forty-five minutes had passed since the battle began, that is, since Captain William Washington and Lieutenant James Monroe had stormed the guardhouse and cut down the sentry. The total American casualties in the battle consisted of two men who were frozen to death on the march and, therefore, could not actually be considered battle casualties; Captain William Washington, shot through both hands when he stormed the guardhouse; and Lieutenant James Monroe, slightly wounded at the same time. There were no dead Americans in the battle.

The Hessians, on the other hand, had suffered much greater losses. The British newspaper reports of the time put the Hessians' loss at about ninety men, but this is very hard to substantiate. Some of those Hessians who had fled deserted and lost themselves in the colonies. Certainly, if they ran from the field of battle and returned to their ranks, they would have been court-martialed and possibly shot for cowardice. It was much easier to lose themselves in America.

30

WASHINGTON STAYED IN THE FIELD. He refused all offers of dry clothing and shelter. He had to know how the battle had finished, and, most of all, he had to convince himself that the battle indeed was over. He was still unaware of what had happened to General Ewing and General Cadwalader. Immediately following the quiet of the battle's end, he sent riders off to bring him news. When the news came, it was inexplicable. General Ewing was supposed to have crossed before daylight a mile below Trenton and to have taken up a position along the Assanpink Creek and then detach forces to cross the creek and advance upon Trenton.

He never showed up, and as a matter of fact, he had never crossed the river. Washington learned this news after the Battle of Trenton was over, and he also learned that Ewing's reason was that there had been too much ice. But most damaging to Washington was the fact that Cadwalader of Philadelphia, a man he had trusted so and had indeed made into a general just before the battle, had failed him. After managing to bring the majority of his troops across the Delaware River about nine miles below Trenton, Cadwalader found it too difficult to load the cannon. Instead of having the courage and the audacity either to come to Washington's assistance or to attack Von Donop, the Hessian leader encamped at Bordentown, Cadwalader reembarked his men and recrossed to the west bank of the Delaware River and safety.

This news was brought to Washington, but he could neither comprehend nor digest it. Washington, who had apparently never known the terror that men can experience in battle, was at a loss to understand or to sympathize with it in others, especially among his own general officers. A private soldier might exhibit fear; in an officer Washington found it unforgivable.

The end of the battle had left him cold as ice, emotionless and depressed. He called grimly for a search of every house, every cellar, every stable in Trenton. He ordered every woodpile turned over. He demanded that all the Hessians in Trenton and in the region around it be taken prisoner and accounted for.

Already, at Mercer's orders, a list of the British losses was being prepared. It would seem from the information they had at hand that Lossberg's regiment had surrendered one lieutenant colonel, one major, one captain, three lieutenants, four ensigns, thirty-eight sergeants, six drummers, nine musicians and nine servants of the officers, with two hundred and six rank and file.

From Rahl's regiment there had been three colonels, a major, a captain, two lieutenants, five ensigns, two surgeon's mates, twenty-five sergeants, three drummers, four musicians, nine servants of officers and two hundred and forty-four of the rank and file.

From Knyphausen's regiment a major and two captains, two lieutenants and three ensigns, twenty-five sergeants, six drummers, six servants of officers and two hundred and fifty-eight of the rank and file.

From the artillery regiment a lieutenant and four sergeants and two servants of officers and thirty-eight of the rank and file.

These were the figures brought to Washington early that day. Later, perhaps, they might be adjusted, but nothing would change the fact that he had taken the vast bag of over nine hundred prisoners, six double-fortified brass three-pound cannon, with carriages complete, three ammunition wagons, twelve drums and all the colors of three Hessian regiments. This last in particular must have given a singular pleasure to the man who had begun to learn the bloody game of war with the slaughter in Brooklyn.

The booty of the great victory went further than Hessian prisoners. There were great piles of muskets, enormous stores of all sorts of military supplies, drums of powder, iron kettles filled with musket balls.

Already the freezing Yankee soldiers were pulling the coats off the Hessians and covering up their own rags. Some of them had found two drums of rum among the Hessian stores. When the first rum was breached, Greene realized that the great victory could still be turned into a fiasco. Rum was the last thing the young soldiers needed, and he confiscated it immediately. By the hundreds the Americans had dropped to the wooden sidewalks and to the muddy streets, sleeping where they fell. Their officers walked among the men, beating them with canes and with the flats of their swords, to get them to stand guard duty over the shivering, defeated Hessians.

Sitting on his horse in something of a daze, Washington moved across the captured town, looking at the booty that was being assembled, piles of thick woolen blankets—his men would be cold no longer—mounds of sheets and linen and scarves and coats and boots. Soldiers watching him wondered afterward why he should have been so deeply depressed and sad, having gained so great and spectacular a victory against all odds, against all reason, against all hopes.

31

GENERAL GREENE RODE UP alongside of Washington, took his arm gently, and said to him, "General Washington, Colonel Rahl is dying."

Washington's response was to the effect that war was always a matter of life and death, and if Rahl was dying, let him damn well die.

Greene argued that Washington could not let Rahl die in this manner, that every dictate of military courtesy urged the commander in chief to go to the Hessian, face him and sympathize with him as gentlemen did with each other, even when they served on opposite sides.

Washington answered to the effect that he wanted no words with any Hessian.

Now Mercer joined them and pressed him to do as Greene suggested. At this point Washington had neither the will nor the strength to argue further, and he rode along with Greene to the Potts house. The house was sealed off by a guard of Pennsylvania riflemen, who opened their ranks to let the commander in chief and Greene through.

Washington and Greene then went upstairs to where Colonel Rahl had been laid out on the bed of the owner of the house. Mr. and Mrs. Potts were in the room and also their daughter, three Hessian officers and a young American lieutenant. Greene, who was a Quaker himself, had hurriedly explained to Washington who the Pottses were and the circumstances that had brought Rahl to the house. Washington did not respond. What Quakers did was their business, not his. He walked into the room and stood with a stony face before Rahl.

Rahl whispered, and his words went unheard. He raised an arm a trifle, and then Washington bent over the bed to hear him. A young noncommissioned Hessian officer wrote down afterward what Rahl said to Washington.

"Meine Männer sind gute tapfere Männer. Berauben Sie sie nicht. Nehmen Sie ihre Waffen, aber lassen Sie ihnen ihr Geld und ihre Würde."

"My men are good brave men. Don't rob them. Take their arms, but leave them their money and their dignity."

Washington listened to the German words without understanding them, and no one dared to translate in the presence of the cold, bitter commander in chief. Mercer came into the room then and bent over Rahl's bed as a doctor does. The Hessian closed his eyes. A moment later Mercer raised his eyelids, and they remained open. Colonel Rahl was dead in a strange, cold land thousands of miles from his home.

Washington stood erect and without speaking walked out of the room. The contest was over. It had begun in New York six months before, and now the score was settled. Never again would the Hessian on American soil be the figure of terror that he had once been; but neither could Washington forget on that day. He was too spent.

Greene and Mercer followed Washington out of the room. Instead of commenting on Rahl's death, Washington said coldly to Greene and to Mercer that their position was untenable. He asked them whether they realized the luck that had surrounded them every inch of the way? Cadwalader and Ewing with their two armies were still on the west bank of the river. Nothing had gone right, and the lunatic miracle that had just taken place should not deceive them. So far as any of them knew, the Hessian Von Donop was leading his army against Trenton at this very moment.

Washington asked Greene where his men were, and Greene replied that they were sleeping. Washington told Greene to wake them up and get them ready to march.

[32]

HE HIMSELF REFUSED to lie down and rest. He mounted his horse again and rode back and forth through the town, giving orders whenever he met one of his general officers or one of the colonels, this division to be responsible for these stores, that division to be responsible for those stores. He met Sullivan and told him that he wanted the army in marching order by noontime. They were to return to the landing place and recross the river to the Pennsylvania shore. His officers listened to this order, as Sullivan did, with astonishment and disbelief. Yet, when they began to protest, the look on his face stopped them. They remained silent and did as he had commanded.

Wherever he went, he asked for Glover. Men directed him, and finally he found Glover together with Colonel Stark. Stark and Glover were on foot now. The New Englanders walked over to the commander in chief, and the three men stood together and talked.

All around them private soldiers, noncommissioned officers and regular officers stopped to watch the three men and listen. Colonel Johnny Stark of the Bennington Rifles was grinning with pleasure and triumph. His clothes were torn. He had lost his fancy white wig, which he affected at that time, and his hair, face and clothes were caked with

mud and blood. He carried no weapon except a big Hessian cutlass that he clutched in his right hand. He shifted it
to his left so that he could offer his right hand to the commander in chief.

He said words to the effect that they had done it.

There was no one, including George Washington, who
could be angry or distant with Johnny Stark of Vermont.
Only Glover was beyond smiles now as he told the tall skinny Virginian that he had heard that they were crossing the
river again.

"Before nightfall," Washington replied.

Glover said that he, his commander, was mad; but then,
in a manner of speaking, they were all mad.

An hour later the army began to march out of Trenton.
They took with them over nine hundred prisoners, six brass
cannon, gun carriages, at least two hundred Hessian horses, wagons of ammunition, food, clothing, blankets, wagons of medicine, indeed, life, victory and the ability to
continue the war.

For how long? As it seemed to them then, forever.

AN
AFTERWORD

BETWEEN THE TWO CROSSINGS of the Delaware River by the army under the leadership of General Washington, only twenty days elapsed, a very small part of a war that lasted eight years.

In making this study, I am proposing that these twenty days were critical to the final success of the war and to the coming into being of the United States of America. Others might argue with this supposition, and no absolute proof can be offered for or against the contention. In any case, if the twenty days were not the ultimate crisis, they were certainly one of the most critical periods of the American Revolution and perhaps one of the few moments that tested to the limits the endurance of the people involved in the central military effort of the rebellion.

At the time of the American Revolution, the thirteen colonies had been settled by a varied and diverse group of people whose interests were far from homogeneous. However, these varying interests coincided in a unity of desire and necessity at a moment in history that enabled them to join themselves together into a single national force that was able to oppose the British Crown, first in a series of actions of civil disorders and finally with armed force.

Roughly, the colonies can be divided into three areas, New England, the central region, and the South. Farming was universal among the three areas, and in each case the non-agricultural forces had their base in agriculture. The New England region was in its commercial complexion mercantile and fishing. In the central or middle area, which included New York, New Jersey and Pennsylvania, there was a grouping of mercantile interests similar to those of New England. But also there was a good deal of industry: iron works, lumber, leather tanning, papermaking, printing and oven works whose kilns were devoted to the production of pottery and bricks. The southern area, from Virginia to Georgia, was for the most part agricultural; and the main cash crop of this area was tobacco, not yet cotton, for this was still prior to the invention of the cotton gin.

The civil dispute between these thirteen colonies and the mother country of England had been going on for a good many years. It is difficult to place one's finger on the precise moment when civil disturbance changed from random acts of annoyance on the part of the colonies to a maturing movement of civil defiance. The colonies had just contributed a very large and efficient force of soldiers, and arms as well, to the war that we remember as the French and Indian War, that part of the conflict between England and France that took place on the American continent.

The local militia of the various colonies had been tried by fire. They had seen regular British and French troops in action, and they were by no means overawed by the performance of the professionals or doubtful of their own capabilities in this field.

In 1764, a year after the war was over, King George and certain members of the British Parliament put forward a demand that the Americans pay for their share of the large English debt that had been incurred. This demand for contributions was sent to the colonial assemblies, where it was rejected with more or less common indignation.

This was the first real crisis in the British assumption that they had the absolute right to tax the Americans, and this was the first large American defiance of an attempt to exercise that right. Both sides of the dispute found their sensibilities exacerbated, and in 1765 the Quartering Act was passed by Parliament out of pique rather than out of any true necessity. The Quartering Act demanded of the colonies that they make their houses available as living quarters for the standing army of British soldiers that were still an occupation force in America.

Indignation over the Quartering Act ran high. When it was followed by the Stamp Act, which put a stamp tax on all newspapers, pamphlets and on a variety of legal documents, the anger of the people in the colonies reached a point that caused rioting and active resistance. Younger people in the colonies, mostly between fourteen and twenty years of age, began the first organization of quasimilitary resistance, called "The Sons of Liberty."

Everywhere in the colonies the Stamp Act brought into being a sort of official colonial indignation. Patrick Henry introduced a resolution into the Virginia Assembly that condemned and denied the right of Parliament to legislate on any internal affairs of the Commonwealth of Virginia.

Massachusetts, a hotbed of anger generated by both the Stamp and the Quartering Acts, called for a Stamp Act Congress, which met in 1765, and this special group issued a Declaration of Rights. The Stamp Act Congress was in actuality the first mechanism for unity that the colonies put forth and also the first sign of a desire for separate government. The resistance against the Stamp Act was sufficient to cause the British prime minister to repeal it. But in the act of repealing it the British felt that they had to make some new assertion of their right in America and their hold over the colonies.

A man called Charles Townshend, who was then the British chancellor of the exchequer, framed a bill that contained a considerable list of new taxes, taxes on lead and painters' colors, paper, oil, wine, glass and tea—indeed taxes that touched almost every area in which the colonists were attempting to establish their own independent manufacturing and importing facilities. The British rationale for these levies was that the duties collected would be used to pay wages of governors and judges functioning in the colonies.

Again in response to this act of the British, a functioning union, however thin, was put together by the colonists, first in the Massachusetts Circular Letter of 1768 and then later in a Virginia resolution condemning the act. Meanwhile, the New York legislature condemned the Quartering Act and refused to supply any living space for British troops, and in response to this, Parliament deprived New York of its legislative rights.

So began the nonmilitary war, in which each side tested the strength of the other and then withdrew if the opposition became too great. At this point, certainly, not even the most radical elements in the colonies thought in terms of severing their connections with the motherland and organizing an independent nation on American soil.

In the same year, 1768, the merchants of Boston met and signed a nonimportation agreement. Under this pact they agreed to stop all imports from England until the obnoxious taxes were repealed. This agreement against importation was a measure that caught the fancy of the other colonies, and the movement around it spread like wildfire. Boycott, it would appear, has always been an American way of protest.

Again, in response to this action, the King of England dissolved the Massachusetts legislature, and a British warship disembarked a regiment of British soldiers for quartering in Boston. Lord North, the British prime minister, tempered the King's anger and was able to bring about the repeal of all taxes except the levy on tea. This was a nominal tax and it was retained simply for the sake of a principle, that is, to demonstrate the right of the British to tax the colonies. But the exacerbation increased, and the Americans seized upon the symbolic tea tax for further steps toward unification. A movement to stop the drinking of tea swept the colonies, and four years later what is remembered as the Boston Tea Party took place in Massachusetts, an attack on a tea cargo that was dumped into the water of the harbor and that led to an increase in the aggressiveness of the radical elements among the colonists.

In 1770, British soldiers in Boston attacked a large crowd that was yelling insults and throwing snowballs. Known as the Boston Massacre, this bloody police action by the British angered many people in Massachusetts. Parliament reacted by passage of the Boston Port Bill, closing the port, and at the same time the commander of the British troops, General Gage, was made the royal governor of Massachusetts.

In 1772, a British revenue cutter, the *Gaspee*, ran ashore in Narragansett Bay. The *Gaspee* had been attempting to enforce the navigation acts, and now, trapped on the reef, it offered an irresistible target for the men of Providence, who attacked the vessel, captured the crew and then burned the ship where it was.

The Crown's government in Massachusetts organized a commission to investigate the matter, and to determine who was responsible, arrest and bring them to trial in England, but this was all a facade of noise and fury. No one was arrested, and the *Gaspee* incident became in a sense the first real act of war on the part of the Americans.

By now the situation in Boston had become so untenable and so filled with opportunities for further provocation that Massachusetts was looked upon throughout the thirteen colonies as the leader of the incipient rebellion. All of these factors and many more served to bring the thirteen colonies together and to convince them that it was necessary to create some mechanism to extend their need for common action. Thus, the first Continental Congress came into being, and it met in Philadelphia on September 5, 1774.

While all these events and others annoyed and frustrated the American colonists, the basic cause of the American Revolution can be summed up briefly.

The explosive force of settlement and growth in America was proceeding at a pace beyond England's ability to cope. The mercantile interests of the North were in an increasing state of competition with similar British interests, who demanded protection.

In the middle colonies the settlers were producing an extraordinary crop of children; the poorest of the colonial farmers appeared to produce the largest families. And as their sons and daughters came to maturity, they pressed westward for land of their own. Without such land, they felt that they could not exist. Vast tracts of hundreds of thousands of acres had been tied up in British Crown grants. The British were nervous and worried about this westward expansion, and, in order to slow it, they turned their already existing alliance with the Indians against the settlers.

In the South, the planters depended for almost all of their wealth upon the proceeds of their tobacco crops, which were sold in Great Britain. In turn the British agents fixed the price of tobacco at rates that kept the great southern planters, of whom George Washington was one, in a condition of almost perpetual land-rich poverty.

It was the coincidence of these conditions that brought the three disparate elements in the colonies together in the alliance that produced the American Revolution.

It is not to be thought that a society of equalitarianism existed among the thirteen colonies. The class differentiation and gap between the enlisted men in the American army and those who constituted the officer corps was far greater than anything we imagine today. Nor was the army kept together by patriotic pressure or by those irritations that had initially moved the colonists into action. Rather the army was a troubled and shifting group in which the various elements in the colonies continued to fight a battle that expressed their class difference and their basic antagonism toward each other.

This was the army over which George Washington, the Virginia planter, was given command. His command lasted for more than seven years, and those years were a period of agony and toil that few other men could have endured. It is not my purpose to glorify George Washington. He has been wrongly glorified, and in the process the entire meaning and color of the man have been lost.

In the few days of his life that I chose to chronicle here I tried to bring out some of the important and viable facets of the man's character. I do not claim to understand his character. Indeed I doubt whether many of his associates who were with him at the time or beside him through all the seven difficult years that the Revolution lasted either knew him well or understood him. He was tied by chains that he had forged and hidden behind walls that he had erected. But there are sufficient glimpses of this gentle and remarkable man for us to wish that he could come alive again and symbolize those principles which he stood for and which are so necessary in our own time.

He took command of the American army in the late spring of 1775. On May 10, the Continental Congress at Philadelphia chose him to be commander in chief. Certain cynical observers of the scene said that the chief factor that occasioned this choice was the beautiful fashion plate he made in his very expensive buff-and-blue uniform. Be this as it may, the Congress chose well, and Washington went north to take command of his army.

The army was in high spirits then. From the first attempt of the British to seize the arms the Americans had stored at Concord, Massachusetts, the war had been an incredible series of, if not American victories, at least American demonstrations of their power. The British army that retreated from Concord, Massachusetts, back to the security of Boston, was hit and harassed all the way and suffered very grievous losses. In Boston, where the Battle of Bunker Hill took place, the British again suffered bloody and unexpected losses, and though they took their objective, they left the Americans with the feeling that the British army could be beaten at will.

When General Washington took command, this feeling had begun to dissipate. As has been shown in an operation that began in Brooklyn and continued in and around Manhattan Island and then in Jersey, the troops George Washington led suffered defeat after defeat.

The army that Washington brought across the Delaware was, many observers thought, in the final stages of disintegration. The cause that he led at that time had been deemed hopeless by most of the sensible men in the colonies. After he had turned the tide at Trenton, the direction was upward, and even though the American forces were defeated many times and even though they endured winter encampments of great privation, such as that at Valley Forge, never again were they in a process of becoming the remnants around a lost cause.

On the other hand, neither did the progress of the war turn into an endless series of triumphs. It is true that two stunning victories followed Trenton—the first at Princeton in New Jersey, only a week later, and the second in the far Northeast through the summer and fall of 1777, where first Johnny Stark sent Burgoyne's troops reeling and then Gates and Arnold defeated him decisively—but these two victories were only a prelude to four years of bitter, heartbreaking war. In battle after battle, Washington's troops were either defeated or left holding bloody and indecisive ground.

In 1777, Washington was defeated at both Brandywine and at Germantown, after which he took the shattered remnants of his army into winter quarters at Valley Forge. Yet bad as his situation was, it was better than a year ago. He had proved to our French allies that Americans could face the British and Hessians, bayonet to bayonet, and win as well as lose. He had captured great stores of booty, so his condition, dreadful as it was, did not ever again approach the point of disintegration that marked the first crossing of the Delaware River; and most of all, he had proven to the financiers of the American cause that ground could be held and battles won and had thereby assured his army of at least minimum financial backing.

Having lived through the winter at Valley Forge, Washington turned to the offensive—as he had eighteen months before—and at the end of June, he attacked General Clinton's army at Monmouth in New Jersey.

Who won or who lost the Battle of Monmouth was of less importance than the fact that it occurred. It was one of those indecisive battles in which neither side could claim either victory or a meaningful defeat of the enemy. The important point is that Washington attacked a great British army—not a small garrison, as at both Trenton and Princeton, but the solid heart of British military strength—and, at least at several points on the battlefield, held his ground and drove the British back.

The war went on. In the west, on the Pennsylvania frontier, two terrible massacres of Americans took place, while the Americans captured the British forts at Vincennes and Kaskaskia. The British moved by sea, and in 1779, they made dozens of incursions and sorties on the coasts of Connecticut, Virginia and the Carolinas. John Paul Jones brought the American navy into being, and fighting from an old hulk, he sank the British warship *Serapis*. In 1780, Gates was badly defeated by Cornwallis in the South, and then a year later, the brilliant and courageous Cornwallis was trapped in the South and destroyed.

Nathanael Greene began the process of Cornwallis's defeat by facing him early in the year, defying him, meeting him and then retreating before him for three hundred miles into the South. When, in August, Cornwallis took up a defensive position at Yorktown, Washington took his army south by forced march, while the French fleet bore down upon Cornwallis by sea.

Out-generaled finally, trapped, General Cornwallis surrendered his army to Washington on the nineteenth of October in 1781, just two months and six days short of five years after the crossing. Two more years would pass before a treaty of peace was finally signed, but to all effects and purposes, the war was over, although some sporadic fighting continued through most of 1782.

Thus, between the crossing and the signing of a treaty of peace, seven years ensued. At the end of that period, very few of the enlisted men who crossed the Delaware with General Washington were still in his army. Many of them were dead, some of wounds suffered in battle, far more of disease and of privation. Many others incurred incurable illness during the war and never truly recovered from these diseases.

It has been estimated that fewer than six thousand American soldiers died in battle during the American Revolution, but more than a hundred thousand died of wounds, in British prisons and of disease, privation and hunger. In the small population of the time, the cost of that war in human suffering was by no means inconsequential. These early volunteers were cooks who prepared the soup and the meat and the other courses of the dinner, but who never sat at the table or ate the food.

A study was once made of the average age of the soldiers in the army Washington led in 1776, and the figure was nineteen years. Like all statistics it tells only a part of the story. To get an average of nineteen years, there had to be hundreds who were no more than fourteen and fifteen and sixteen. These were the boys who had gone forth with high hopes and with brave hearts. The emotion that drew them was simple and uncomplicated. They were defending the land where they had been born and upon which they stood and for most of them the ground that they broke to plant and harvest their crops.

They knew little of war, nor did they make a fetish out of military glory. Quite to the contrary, the sere Protestant ethic that came out of the faith most of them espoused looked upon the European game of war, where men were moved like pawns and sacrificed without qualm or regret, as sin and evil beyond justification.

Most of their names are remembered only in dusty regimental files stored in the basements of various libraries and antiquarian societies, and even the memory of their individual names brings neither profit nor glory to those who died so young. Like most dead, they ask quietly for understanding and for no more than that. No one can speak for them. But one can say that we sin against them if we take their names in vain, and the taking of their names in vain is unfortunately all too easy and glib a part of our day-to-day life in this time in which I write.

However, some of those who were with Washington,

particularly among his immediate circle of officers, must be mentioned in terms of their subsequent actions and fate. Nathanael Greene in particular grew in skill and in stature as the war went on. He became perhaps the finest, the most intellectual and the most intrepid military commander on the Continental side. It was owing to his acumen and understanding of the forces he led as well as those he fought against that the great victory at Yorktown in 1781 was achieved.

A word more must be said of John Glover, who led the New England fishermen regiments. The officers of the American Revolution were for the most part educated men who were of the middle class and who owned property. However, among them were many exceptions, as for example, General Greene and John Glover. A shoemaker, later a fisherman, a very plain, outspoken New England man, he was a thorn in the side of the officers of General Washington's staff. He did not like them; they did not like him. Unlike Lee and Gates he was neither a gossip nor a conspirator. If anything, his tendency was to say very little indeed. But he led a brigade of New England fishermen and sailors who were dependable and efficient in what they knew how to do. And he despised the inefficiency and the foolishness that was a part of so much of the American army's efforts during the first two years of the war. In particular he made an enemy of the Boston bookseller, Henry Knox, who was general of artillery and who belonged to the inner circle around General Washington.

During the two generations that followed the American Revolution, there was an outpouring of laudatory accounts purportedly describing what had happened. These accounts were concerned far less with the truth of history than with the ennoblement of everyone who took part in the American Revolution and who fitted into the slot that they labeled patriot. It was during this time that John Glover was eclipsed and indeed to some extent read out of history by a new group of Boston authorities who had taken for themselves and for their own historical privilege the history of the American Revolution.

Ultimately a bronze statue of John Glover was erected on Commonwealth Avenue in Boston. But even today the histories of the period fail to comprehend fully the role that he and his seamen played. The army that was thrown together in 1775 and 1776 was far from a professional army. Years later the remnants of this army, stiffened by the enlistment of thousands of new men, many of them from Pennsylvania, became the finest military force in the Western Hemisphere. It can be said that in 1783, just before its disbandment, the army of the thirteen colonies was more effective and better trained as a military instrument than the troops of any European country.

This training was the result of the years of war that the American army had endured and that had seen it shaped as a fighting force. Yet these years of war could not have taken place without the role played by Colonel Glover and the regiments he commanded.

John Sullivan, the lawyer who had taken command after the capture of General Lee, was sent by Washington into the Mohawk and Genesee Valleys to meet the threat posed by Butler's Tory Rangers and the Indians he led. Sullivan held the frontier and comported himself well. After the war, he became governor of New Hampshire. He died in New Hampshire in his fifty-fifth year.

William Alexander, Lord Stirling, remained with the army as long as his health permitted. Then, ill, and despondent at leaving a struggle to which he had committed himself so wholly, he returned to his home in Albany. He died in 1783, the year the war ended.

Like so many of his time, Henry Knox was short-lived, and he died in 1806 at the age of fifty-six. Throughout his life, his girth increased, nor did he ever waver from his single purpose, to serve Washington in any manner the Virginian desired. Perhaps he was fortunate, for few men live most of their lives with an idol that remains unshattered. He became secretary of war under the Articles of Confederation and then served in Washington's cabinet, hiding whatever inner man there was under a façade of jolly fat-man mirth.

John Cadwalader, the man who turned back after crossing the river, was cleared of charges of treason brought against him and also of charges of cowardice directed at him. In April of 1777 he became Brigadier General of all the Pennsylvania Militia, thus paying a very small price indeed for his desertion of Washington on that morning in 1776.

Of that other man who failed to cross the Delaware, very little is known. Brigadier General James Ewing disappears from history and from the minds of Americans, perhaps a fate that he justly deserved. We know that he fought under Braddock in the French and Indian War and that he was made Brigadier General of Pennsylvania Militia. But who was he actually? In his memoirs, Wilkinson remembers him as General Irvin. William S. Stryker, as puzzled as most historians, quotes a Dr. Gordon who calls the General

"Erwing." Thomas Marshall, an officer of the army, refers to him as Irvine, and Washington refers to him hardly at all.

General Gates went on with his plotting and his cliquism. Even though in 1777 he won national fame for his victory at Saratoga, he could never nurture his soldiers' admiration into love. The so-called Conway Cabal, which had as its intention the replacement of Washington with Gates as commander in chief, came to nothing. In 1780 Gates suffered a bitter defeat at the Battle of Camden. He was removed from his post of commander of his army and replaced by Nathanael Greene. Two years later a congressional committee was organized to investigate him but then canceled the investigation before it ever took place. Forgotten, he died in New York City in 1806.

The two young aides of General Washington, James Monroe and Alexander Hamilton, made their own mark on history, the one to become President of the United States, the other to achieve a short but brilliant career that was terminated finally by Aaron Burr.

Young Captain William Washington, that distant cousin—possibly—of the commander in chief, fought brilliantly through the war. A big, easygoing, good-natured young man, with the open cherubic face of a well-fed boy and the body of a professional athlete, he established no claim for service and drifted out of history easily and comfortably.

General Charles Lee, that one-time companion of General Gates, was exchanged for a British officer and given his command again. At the Battle of Monmouth he led a retreat that George Washington intercepted, and there on the battlefield Washington cursed him roundly, beat him with the flat of his sword and to all effects brought his career to an end. Subsequently, documents came to light that revealed a treasonable relationship between General Charles Lee and General Howe, the British commander, in which Lee would aid Howe to capture the city of Philadelphia.

Lee was court-martialed for disobeying orders and suspended from service for a year. His abuse of Washington caused John Laurens, an admirer of Washington, to challenge him to a duel, out of which they both emerged alive. In 1780, he was dismissed from military service by Congress, and from there on his life moves into the shadows; little is known of the two years remaining to him before he died.

General Hugh Mercer, Washington's best and closest friend, died of a bullet wound a few days after the Battle of Trenton at the Battle of Princeton, for Washington had paused only to regroup his forces and then had crossed the river again to attack and defeat the British garrison at Princeton.

Johnny Stark of Vermont lived on to be ninety-four years old. Perhaps more than any of his companions, he lived a life of fullness and fulfillment. He died in the twilight of his years in his beloved Vermont.

And finally that most colorful of the young officers serving under George Washington, James Wilkinson, whom I took the liberty of paraphrasing frequently, deserves some space; for his certainly was the strangest of all careers. After the Battle of Trenton, he rejoined General Gates and with Gates plotted against his commander in chief to an extent where even Congress censured him publicly. In spite of this censure Congress promoted him to the rank of brigadier general in 1777, when he was only twenty years old according to some records and twenty-three according to others, for nothing concerning Wilkinson was ever the absolute truth.

He was the confidence man supreme, and so eloquent in conveying his own virtues that in 1778 the Continental Congress made him secretary of the board of war. He had to resign this post because of the scandal of his involvements with General Gates in the Conway Cabal. By 1779 he had become clothier general of the army, a position he held for two years. During that time he had apparently stolen so much money in his connivances with tailors that he was forced to resign. Finally, feeling a need to remove himself from the public eye, Wilkinson went to Kentucky, and by 1782 he was accepting bribes for the purpose of making the state of Kentucky a bastion of Mexico. He built a most notorious reputation among the western conspirators who were intriguing for a connection with Mexico and secession from the new United States of America as a way to gain Spanish ports for American shipping.

The most remarkable feature of Wilkinson was his adroitness. By 1791 he had slid his way out of the scandals and conspiracies he had been involved in and reentered the army. When Anthony Wayne died in 1796, Wilkinson became the ranking officer of the American army. He was still taking pay from the Spaniards when as governor of the Louisiana territory in 1805 he entered, with Aaron Burr, into a scheme for dividing the western half of the United States from the mother country. Then after some plotting and further consideration, Wilkinson decided that it would be more profitable to betray Burr than to befriend him.

Having made this decision, Wilkinson went to Thomas Jefferson and revealed to him all the details of Burr's conspiracy. Wilkinson then became the prosecution's chief witness at Burr's trial. The defense attorneys argued, and with some justification, that Wilkinson had spent his life betraying every trust that was ever reposed in him. In spite of all this he managed to have himself cleared by an army board of inquiry. The rest of his life played out like a comic opera of fraud and deceit. Many of his contemporaries remembered him with delight as the scoundrel par excellence.

The Hessian officers were less fortunate in their future, and they were less easily forgotten. The court-martial that they all eventually had to face was far more stringent in its verdicts than the Congress of the United States in its judgments of American officers who had failed in their efforts. The Hessians succumbed to the common human characteristic of blaming the dead, since the dead are voiceless, and the accusation against Colonel Rahl by his fellow officers was "dereliction of duty."

Lieutenant Piel, one of the officers who fought with the Hessians and who took part in the court-martial, eventually wrote his story of what had occurred in Trenton. Here is the Hessian lieutenant's account, translated by Washington Irving:

For our whole ill luck we have to thank Colonel Rall [*sic*]. It never occurred to him that the rebels might attack us; and, therefore, he had taken scarce any precautions against such an event. In truth, I must confess we have universally thought too little of the rebels, who, until now, have never on any occasion been able to withstand us.

Our Brigadier [Rahl] was too proud to retire a step before such an enemy, although nothing remained for us but to retreat.

General Howe had judged this man from a wrong point of view, or he would hardly have entrusted such an important post as Trenton to him. He was formed for a soldier, but not for a general. At the capture of Fort Washington he had gained much honor while under the command of a great general, but he lost all his renown at Trenton where he himself was General. He had the courage to dare the hardiest enterprise; but he alone wanted the cool presence of mind necessary in a surprise like that at Trenton. His vivacity was too great; one thought crowded on another, so that he could come to no decision. Considered as a private man, he was deserving of high regard. He was generous, open-handed, hospitable; never cringing to his superiors, nor arrogant to his inferiors; but courteous to all. Even his domestics were treated more like friends than servants.

My own judgment of Colonel Rahl would be more generous than Lieutenant Piel's. From all I can gather from various conflicting statements about the battle, Lieutenant Piel, who was close to or in the guardhouse that was attacked by William Washington and James Monroe, more easily lost his nerve and his presence of mind than did Colonel Rahl. In fairness, it should be remembered that Colonel Rahl kept his head and that as long as he was alive the tide of battle appeared to have turned in favor of the Hessians.

Rahl was buried in Trenton in the graveyard of the Presbyterian church. On his gravestone it was written:

"Hier liegt der Oberst Rahl
Mit ihm ist alles all!"

("Here lies Colonel Rahl
For him, all is over.")

The Hessian officers were exchanged for American officers who were captives of the British. Eventually all of
those who survived the Battle of Trenton returned either to
various commands in the Hessian units that were with the
British army in America or back to Hesse to retire from the
service.

Time has decked the Hessians with a great many characteristics that have little relationship to the truth. We are
all too ready, under the influence of the First and Second
World Wars, to compare the Hessian mercenaries to Hitler's
troops, but such a comparison is totally fallacious. The Hessians were professional soldiers of the eighteenth century,
and they had all of the best and all of the worst features of
such mercenaries. It was not until the French Revolution
that the notion of a man fighting for the defense of his own
nation as a volunteer matured into a justification of a military career for enlisted men.

In truth the Hessians were no different from the British
or French soldiers or the soldiers of any other German state.
The Landgrave of Hesse-Cassel had developed a small but
well-trained army that was considered one of the very best
on the European continent. The army was in great demand
for mercenary service by the various European sovereigns.
The men in this army were not slaves but volunteer soldiers,
who sought mercenary status as a means of bettering their
condition. This is not a moral judgment but simply a statement of fact. When the King of France sent his troops to
America to fight on the side of the Americans, they were
mercenaries like the Hessians who were fighting on the side

of the British. This must be seen clearly in order to understand the position of the Hessians in America.

Certainly King Louis of France was far more of a tyrant than the Landgrave of Hesse-Cassel, and certainly French soldiers had as little interest in the American cause as the Hessian soldiers had in the British cause. The fact is that in 1776, except for the Americans, every army in the Western world was made up of mercenaries. Small nations like Switzerland or Hesse, unable to engage in blood baths of their own devising, hired out their soldiers to larger nations who could better afford the brigandage of war. But it is unrealistic to believe that the British regular—who would fire his musket in any direction ordered—gave one small damn as to whether the Continental soldiers were free or a part of the Empire.

The Hessians were well paid and outfitted and usually well fed. If married and without child, they were allowed to bring their wives on campaign with them, and this was the case with hundreds of Hessian soldiers in America. Man for man, they were superior both in the quality of their soldiering and in their pride in their service to the British soldier of the line.

Though the Hessian officers were exchanged for American officers and went back into the ranks of the British army or home to their own land, no such good fortune awaited the Hessian soldiers, that is, the Hessian rank and file who were taken prisoners at Trenton. Hundreds of them were sold into servitude as chattel slaves, to do forced labor in the iron works at Durham, the same iron works that had created the Durham boats that Washington used to cross the Delaware. They were bought by the forge owners for thirty Spanish dollars per man, and others were sold to the Pennsylvania charcoal burners to clear forests and create fuel for the furnaces. Still other Hessian soldiers were indentured to American farmers at the price of eighty Spanish dollars per Hessian couple, man and wife. This indenture was for a period of three years, and during those years the Hessians were virtual slaves, their lot in no way superior to the fate of any black slave in America at that time.

They were, however, given an alternative. They were told that as prisoners of war they were free to enter the American army, where their military knowledge would be valued and respected. Hessian officers were offered one hundred acres of land if they would enlist in the American ranks.

Many Hessians availed themselves of this opportunity. Others, who were sold into indentured servitude, escaped. There is in German a very considerable literature of the adventures of these Hessians in the American forests as they sought their way back to their own regiments and of the hardships they endured. Many, including some with their wives, made their way through the wilderness and survived to rejoin their regiments and eventually returned to Hesse-Cassel.

The records show that a total of 16,992 Hessians were brought to America. Of this number, 10,492 returned to Europe in 1783. No exact figures are available. However, we can take it as very close to the historical fact that 6,500 Hessians who came to America remained. Some of them were killed or wounded, and perhaps some of them died of their injuries, but most of them became American citizens and made their lives here.

Bibliography

Adams, James Truslow. *Revolutionary New England*. Atlantic-Little Brown; Boston, 1923

Andrews, Charles M. *The Colonial Period of American History*. 4 vols. Yale U. Press; New Haven, 1934, 1938

Beard, Charles and Mary. *The Rise of American Civilization*. Macmillan; N.Y., 1930

Bedini, Silvio A. *Ridgefield in Review*. The Ridgefield 250th Anniversary Comm., Ridgefield, Conn., 1958

Billias, George Athan. *General John Glover*. Holt, Rinehart & Winston; N.Y., 1960

——. *George Washington's Opponents*. William Morrow; N.Y., 1969

Burnett, Edmund C. *The Continental Congress*. Macmillan; N.Y., 1941

Commager, Henry Steele and Morris, Richard B. *The Spirit of 'Seventy-Six*. 2 vols. Bobbs Merrill; Indianapolis and N.Y., 1958

Curtis, Edward E. *The Organization of the British Army in the American Revolution*. Yale U. Press; New Haven, 1926

Fast, Howard. *The Selected Work of Tom Paine*. Duell, Sloan & Pearce; N.Y., 1945

Fisher, Sydney George. *The True History of the American Revolution*. J. B. Lippincott Co.; Phila., 1903

——. *The Struggle for American Independence*. J. B. Lippincott Co.; Phila., 1908

Fisk, John. *The American Revolution.* 2 vols. Houghton Mifflin; Boston, 1891

Hammond, Otis G., ed. *The Sullivan Papers.* New Hampshire Historical Society Publications; Concord, 1930–1939

Harlow, Ralph V. "Some Aspects of Revolutionary Finances." *American Historical Review,* Vol. 35. N.Y., 1934

Harwood, Paul Leland. *George Washington, Country Gentleman.* Bobbs-Merrill; Indianapolis and N.Y., 1925

Historical Register of Officers of the Continental Army. Heitman, 1917

Hughes, Rupert. *George Washington; the Human Being and the Hero.* William Morrow; N.Y., 1926

Irving, Washington. *The Life of George Washington.* Putnam; N.Y., 1868

Lefferts, Charles M. *Uniforms of the American, British, French and German Armies in the War of the American Revolution.* The New York Historical Society, 1926

Miller, John C. *Sam Adams.* Atlantic-Little Brown and Co.; Boston, 1936

——. *Origins of the American Revolution.* Atlantic-Little Brown and Co.; Boston, 1943

——. *Triumph of Freedom.* Atlantic-Little Brown and Co.; Boston, 1948

Moore, George H. *The Treason of Charles Lee.* Charles Scribner; N.Y., 1860

Morris, Richard B. *The Era of the American Revolution.* Columbia U. Press; N.Y., 1939

Morrison, S. E. and Commager, H. S. *The Growth of the American Republic.* Oxford U. Press; N.Y., 1937

Pennypacker, Morton. *General Washington's Spies.* Long Island Historical Society; Bklyn, N.Y., 1939

Rosengarten, J. G. *The German Allied Troops 1776–1783.* J. Munsell; Albany, 1893

Spaulding, Oliver L. *The United States Army in War and Peace.* Putnam; N.Y., 1937

Stryker, William S. *The Battles of Trenton and Princeton.* Houghton Mifflin; Boston, 1898

Thane, Elswyth. *Potomac Squire.* Duell, Sloan & Pearce; N.Y., 1963

Van Doren, Carl. *Benjamin Franklin.* Viking Press; N.Y., 1938

——. *Secret History of the American Revolution.* Viking Press; N.Y., 1941

Wilkinson, James. *Memoirs of My Own Times.* Abraham Small; Phila., 1816

REFERENCES:

Archives of Pennsylvania.

Archives of the State of New Jersey.

Dictionary of American Biography. 20 vols. Charles Scribner; N.Y., 1928

Harper's Encyclopedia of United States History. 10 vols. Harper Bros.; N.Y., 1907

In addition to the above, I have made good use of the library at the Memorial Building at Washington Crossing State Park, in Bucks County, Pennsylvania. The people there have been kind and helpful in their knowledge of the local geography and of the immediate riverside in relation to the crossing. There, one has full freedom to examine every detail of the Durham boat, reconstructed as a part of the park.

I must also acknowledge the kindness of the people in the Thompson-Neely house and their willingness to answer questions. Pamphlets, maps and reproductions of old material, for sale and given away at each of the above places, have also been useful.

And, of course, I must acknowledge the help of my wife, who patiently and uncomplainingly traveled these old paths, joined my attempts to find old ghosts, so long gone, prowled with me around Baskingridge and a dozen other Jersey towns, painstakingly examined miles of the Delaware River, and served as secretary and researcher.

Most of this research, however, served as background material. A great deal of directly pertinent material had been detailed by James Wilkinson, William S. Stryker and Washington Irving. It is true that Wilkinson saw all events in his own reflection, and that neither Irving nor Stryker was critical or even wholly realistic about the men who played the major roles in this story. Neither of them even alluded, for example, to Lord Stirling's drinking—or "drunkenness" as so many of his contemporaries put it—or to Stephen's black temper and frequent bouts of drunkenness, or to Ewing and Cadwalader's only too apparent cowardice; for these were men whose loyalty was accepted as covering all weaknesses. Also, it is most difficult to make any truthful judgments of men in so contentious a situation, where even saints would produce enemies.

But in terms of the major currents of my story, Irving and Stryker did magnificent if old-fashioned work of reconstruction, and of course I leaned upon them heavily.

Where original facts emerged, they were not very important to my story. For instance, lunching one day at the old inn at New Hope, the charming owner told my wife and me a story of a letter recently uncovered by a local inhabitant that indicated that Washington had a meeting in the same place on the fifteenth or sixteenth of December in 1776. But although this was a wholly new piece of material, the letter could offer little that was new to the tale. The writings of Thomas Paine were of great value, and Henry Steele Commager and Richard B. Morris had selected for their very fine book, *The Spirit of 'Seventy-Six*, most of the pertinent and colorful documentary material of that incident, making access to this material so much the easier for any researcher.

A meticulous examination of the Pennsylvania and New Jersey archives revealed six or seven items that Stryker had not used—all of them pleas for food, medicine and clothes.

Originally, my hope had been to uncover enough material excitingly pertinent to the *crossing* to make a more detailed study than this, but the paucity of information in the Philadelphia newspapers was incredible. I was able to extract a few items from the newspapers, but there was nothing available comparable to the New England newspapers of the time, which offer enough intriguing information to make a history of the war in New England with no other sources.

The reason for this is that before the crossing took place, the depression and despair were so great as to discourage writing what amounted to an obituary, and Philadelphia, naturally, was wholly concerned with its own salvation. The few dismal, awful weeks on the Delaware were speedily forgotten and subordinated to the military events that followed.

NOTES FOR *The First Crossing* (East *to* West)

NOTES: *Chapter* 1

Both the British retreat from Concord and the subsequent Battle at Breed's Hill (commonly remembered as Bunker Hill) in Boston convinced the Yankee Continental that the British were not only mortal but stupid. At the same time, the more sensitive in the American ranks realized that Bunker Hill was a psychological error that might never be repeated; while the fierce infighting of the British, when pressed, might be repeated all too often. There, too, the British use of the bayonet as a terrible and deadly weapon was felt for the first time, as remarked upon in a letter written by Sir William Howe to his adjutant general and quoted by Fortescue, who is quoted by Sidney George Fisher:

"Pigott was relieved from his enemies in that quarter, and in the 2nd onset he carried the redoubt in the handsomest manner, tho' it was most obstinately defended to the last. Thirty of the Rebels not having time to get away were killed with bayonets in it."

NOTES: *Chapter* 2

A whole body of mythology has grown up around the long rifles that were introduced from the Austrian Tyrol in 1730 and manufactured by talented gunsmiths in Pennsylvania in Colonial times, particularly at Lancaster and Philadelphia and somewhat later in Kentucky. In Pennsylvania, many of these rifles were made by German gunsmiths, and each was a work of art. They were accurate at a longer range than any musket, and in the hands of a fine marksman, they were an excellent hunting weapon.

But they were not called "squirrel guns" without reason. Their small bullet was frequently ineffective against larger game, and once fired, they were reloaded only with the greatest of difficulty, the bullet having to be pounded into the small rifle bore. Because of this, almost no body of militia was armed with these guns, and the corollary was that those divisions of riflemen enlisted in the Continental army were undrilled, makeshift and undisciplined. The very fact that so many of them were footloose hunters mitigated against the quality of steadiness desired.

The story of Colonel (later General) John Glover remained obscure until George Athan Billias wrote his excellent biography, *General John Glover and His Marblehead Mariners*. Since Glover plays so large a role in my own work, the use of the above background material is general. Also, for Glover, see the Marblehead town records, American Archives, fourth and fifth series.

NOTES: *Chapter 5*

Lafayette, in his memoirs, Volume I, p. 19, London, 1887, provides the following interesting description of a section of the Continental army:

"About eleven thousand men ill armed, and still worse clothed, presented a strange spectacle. Their clothes were particolored and many of them were almost naked. The best clad wore hunting shirts, large grey linen coats which were much used in Carolina. As to their military tactics, it will be sufficient to say that, for a regiment ranged in battle order to move forward on the right of its line it was necessary for the left to make a continued counter-march. They were always arranged in two lines, the smallest men in the first line."

While we specify a colonel in command of a regiment or battalion, he would have a lieutenant colonel and a major as his staff officers in command. The rest of his staff would include a surgeon with one or two or three surgeon's mates, a quartermaster and an adjutant. Often enough, the local Congregational or Presbyterian minister would come along as chaplain, and since the surgeon was an educated man—a gentleman in the class terms of the time—he would frequently double as commander.

The companies would have a sergeant for every twenty men—in their first organization—and each sergeant would be assisted by two to four corporals. There would be music provided by as many fifers and drummer boys each company could enlist. In the first year of the war, the drummer boys were frequently as young as twelve and thirteen years, the soldiers sometimes as young as fourteen.

In New England, the companies numbered from fifty-nine to seventy-nine men—a curious number given in the documents of the time—even though the Provincial Congress had fixed the number of company men at one hundred. Ideally, the regiment would consist of ten companies, or one thousand men, and the brigade of ten regiments, or ten thousand men. In all truth, most companies were limited to a few dozen, regiments to a few hundred at best, and brigades to little more than a thousand.

NOTES: *Chapter* 6

Few accounts of the American Revolution mention the role played by the Scottish Highlanders and their terrifying effect upon the young American recruits as they advanced behind their skirling pipes; in particular, the 42nd Royal Highland Regiment, later made famous by Kipling as the "Black Watch." This regiment was curiously armed during the Brooklyn and Manhattan Island campaign, in that each man carried in addition to musket and bayonet an enormous sword, not unlike the old Scottish claymore. In the heat of battle, the Highlanders were wont to cast aside musket and bayonet and go berserk, laying about them with their huge swords. Even though these swords were abandoned toward the end of 1776, the legend of fear they had created went with the Highland regiments. It was difficult enough to teach the farm boys in the American ranks to face bayonets; broadswords swung by battle-crazed Highlanders were too much.

Several kilted Highland regiments were raised among the Tory colonists, as for example the North Carolina Highland Regiment, which was under the command of Lt. Colonel Alexander Stewart. This regiment was entirely raised in the colonies, out of loyalists. Another Highland regiment, kilted and in full Highland regalia, pipes and all, was the Royal Highland Emigrants, commanded by Lt. Colonel John Small—also raised in the colonies.

There were at least twelve regiments of Orangemen raised in the colonies to fight for the British—King's Orange Rangers, Volunteers of Ireland, Loyal Irish Volunteers, to mention only a few—and several of them wore the kilt and used pipers.

It is all too little remembered today how much of the American Revolution was a civil war. In the course of the Revolution, the British were able to raise eighty-two regiments of foot soldiers and cavalry in the colonies and in Canada, and while most of these troops were far from dependable in terms of enlistment, they do indicate the extent to which the population of the colonies was ideologically split.

That Washington had a personal bodyguard of black soldiers is often glossed over, as is the fact of so many black volunteers in the American ranks; but black regiments among the British is something only to be surmised. We have the record of a British regiment called "The Black Volunteers," commanded by Captain George Martin, and one might guess that it was composed of escaped slaves—but proof requires a good deal of additional research.

NOTES: *Chapter 7*

It is impossible to put together any clear account of the extent of General Washington's artillery in the summer of 1776. However, it is likely that the Continental army owned more than three hundred cannon of various caliber before the Battle of Long Island. No better impression of the retreat can be given than simply to state that by the time the army reached the Delaware River, less than twenty cannon remained in its possession.

NOTES: *Chapter 8*

There has been much argument concerning Paine's status with the American army at that time. Washington Irving implies that Washington gave him some sort of temporary rank, and this is possible, so loosely were ranks awarded. Some such rank would have helped Paine to explain his presence, since the notion of a war correspondent remained in the future.

NOTES: *Chapter 9*

The following material on the Durham boats has been prepared by the researchers at Washington Crossing State Park, in Pennsylvania. Curiously enough, the fact and function of these boats in a precise sense has been somewhat obscure until recent years. Now, a facsimile of one of the original boats has been built and placed in a cradle on the west bank of the Delaware River near the crossing point. Its great size and weight is surprising at first, and it appears incredible that these huge craft—reminiscent of Viking ships—could be manhandled across an icy river.

Although today most people identify the Durham Boat as the type used in the famous painting, "Washington Crossing the Delaware," actually, from Colonial times and for a hundred years afterward, it had an interesting history of its own.

In Bucks County in the hills near Riegelsville, iron ore was discovered in 1727. The Durham Iron Works which established itself there had a very special kind of boat built in 1750 to carry heavy loads of ore and pig iron down the treacherous rapids of the Delaware River to market in Philadelphia. A great river traffic grew up around this type of boat, which continued to be known as the Durham Boat. At one time 2000 rivermen ran more than 300 Durham Boats from Easton to Philadelphia, hauling iron and grain, whiskey and local produce downstream, and light loads of manufactured goods upstream. When the boats docked, during the period 1750–1860, scenes around the saloons of Easton, Trenton and Philadelphia were often as lively as any in the Old West.

Durham Boats varied in length from forty to sixty feet. One forty feet in length with an eight foot beam and a depth of hold of about three feet, six inches, would have a draft of 5 inches when empty, and when loaded with 15 tons, about 30 inches. The current carried it downstream, while a crew of six men and a captain wielded the steering sweep, 25 to 30 feet long, and the setting poles and oars to guide it over the rapids. Upstream only two or three tons were carried and the boat was poled along from the bottom of the riverbed.

Such boats were used by General George Washington for the famous crossing of the Delaware, Christmas night, 1776. After he had crossed to Pennsylvania early in December, he began his plan for recrossing toward victory, and used his meager funds to buy and hire Durham boats for this purpose.*

In a letter by General Washington, dated December 1, 1776, he wrote, "The boats all along the Delaware River should be secured, particularly the Durham Boats." Such boats should be capable of carrying horses and cannon, as well as men, and when the fateful night came they were manned by General Glover's Marblehead, Mass., fishermen who poled men and equipment safely through the icy river to the Jersey shore. The resultant victory at Trenton on the morning of December 26, 1776, became America's first as a nation.

NOTES: *Chapter* 13

The end pages of the documentary history of the American Revolution, assembled and edited by Henry Steele Commager and Richard B. Morris and published by Bobbs-Merrill in 1958, show a colorful parade of sixteen different uniforms worn by soldiers in the Continental army. This is the work of the book designer, not the editors, who were fully aware that most uniforms of the American Revolution consisted of *decoration after the fact*, sometimes a hundred years after the fact. Apart from uniforms made for themselves by affluent officers or by well-to-do city companies, there were almost no uniforms at all. Regarding the "hunting shirt," we have this interesting comment from *Force*, fifth series, Volume I, p. 676:

"The General [Washington], sensible of the difficulty and expense of providing clothes of almost any kind for the troops, feels an unwillingness to recommend, much more to order, any kind of uniform; but as it is absolutely necessary that the men should have clothes, and appear decent and tight, he earnestly encourages the use of hunting shirts, with long breeches made of the same cloth, gaiter-fashion about the legs, to all those yet unprovided."

*This is not correct. The boats were commandeered for the army.

On July 24, 1776, Washington issued an order recommending hunting shirts for all troops.

Southeastern Pennsylvania had been for years a center of refuge and settlement for German religious dissenters. By this time, there were many established settlements of Mennonites, Moravians and Lutherans. The Moravians were Germanized Bohemians, followers of John Huss, with a long tradition of resistance to oppression. The Pennsylvania Germans provided many regiments of troops for General Washington's army, and they fought through the war with steadiness and devotion. The Moravians in particular provided medical services, nursing, and so much food that they often went hungry themselves.

NOTES: *Chapter* 15

I have seen several accounts of General Israel Putnam's intransigeance and cruelty, qualities which went with his rock-like dependability. Some might argue that such is virtue in the ultimate horror of war, but Washington and many of his staff officers were able to fight and come to victory without those qualities of heartlessness.

The following, from Bedini's fascinating *Ridgefield in Review*, is to the above point:

Among the papers of Lieutenant Samuel Richards, paymaster in Colonel Wylly's regiment, was the following account:

"Feb. 4, 1779. Was tried at a general Court Martial Edward Jones for Going to and serving the enemy, and coming out as a spy—found guilty of each and every charge Exhibited against him, and according to the Law and Usages of Nations was sentenced to suffer death.

"The General (Putnam) approves the sentence and orders it to be put in execution between the hours of ten and eleven A.M. by hanging him by the neck till he be DEAD."

Two days later a soldier of the First Connecticut Regiment was tried and found guilty of desertion to the enemy, and General Putnam ordered the two prisoners to be executed at the same time. Accordingly, the hill which rose above and beyond the American camp (now known as Gallows Hill) was selected for the execution and a gallows was erected. Barber related that the hangman absconded and several boys about twelve years of age were ordered by Putnam to serve in his place. Jones was compelled to ascend a ladder to the gallows, which was about twenty feet from the ground. After the rope had been placed about his neck, General Putnam ordered him to jump from the ladder. Jones refused, however, and stated that he was not guilty of the crime with which he was charged. Putnam then reportedly ordered the boys to overturn the ladder, and, upon their refusal, forced them to do so at the point of his sword . . .

NOTES: *Chapter* 18

General Washington and the Continental Congress saw the struggle very differently. Though Congress was ready to concede immediate if not ultimate hopelessness, Washington would not admit more than a temporary difficulty. His refusal to admit defeat at this low point is well illustrated in the following exchange of correspondence, as quoted by William S. Stryker, *The Battles of Trenton and Princeton*, Houghton Mifflin and Company, 1898. The letter is dated December 12, 1776.

"To Colonel Cadwalader: You are to post your Brigade at and near Bristol. Colonel Nickerson's Regiment to continue where it is at Dunk's ferry but if you find from reconnoitering the ground, or from any movements of the enemy, that any other disposition is necessary, you'll make it accordingly without waiting to hear from me, but to acquaint me with the alterations and the reasons for it as soon as possible. You'l [*sic*] establish the necessary guards and throw up some little redoubts at Dunk's ferry and the different passes in the Neshamine.

"Pay particular attention to Dunk's ferry as its' [*sic*] not improbable that something may be attempted there. Spare no pains or expense to get intelligence of the enemies [*sic*] motions and intentions. Any promises made, or sums advanced, shall be fully complied with and discharged. Keep proper Patrols going from guard to guard. Every piece of intelligence you obtain worthy notice, send it forward by express. If the enemy attempts a landing on this side you'l [*sic*] give them all the opposition in your power. Should they land between Trenton Falls and Bordentown ferry or anywhere above Bristol, and you find your force quite unequal to their force give them what opposition you can at Neshamine ferry and fords. In a word you are to give them all the opposition you can without hazzarding [*sic*] the loss of your Brigade."

On the same day Washington wrote to General Ewing as follows: "Sir:—Your Brigade is to guard the river Delaware from the ferry opposite to Bordentown until you come within two miles or thereabouts of Yardley's Mill to which General Dickinson's will extend.

"About one hundred or a hundred and fifty men will I think be sufficient at the post opposite to Bordentown. The principal part of your force should be as convenient as possible to the ford above Holp's Mill in order that if a passage should be attempted at that place you may be able to give the earliest and most spirited opposition; the success of which depending upon good intelligence and the vigilance [*sic*] of your guards and sentrys [*sic*] will induce you to use every means in your power to procure the first and every endeavor to enforce and encourage the latter."

Washington then goes on to say as he did to Cadwalader: "Spare no pains nor costs to gain information of the enemies [*sic*] movements and designs. Whatever sums you pay to obtain this end I will cheerfully refund. Every piece of information worthy of communication transmit to me without loss of time."

It is interesting to note the stress that Washington places upon payment for information. Apparently he is not then under the spell of a mythology of so-called patriotism that is to entwine itself in after-years around the people who were involved in the Revolution as spies.

The third communication, not unlike the above two, was sent to General Dickinson, whose troops were guarding the area around Yardley's Ferry. Washington had decided that an attitude of defense must contain within itself the greatest mobility possible, so few were his troops, and he wrote to General Dickinson as he had written to both Ewing and Cadwalader, as follows:

"See the troops always have three days' provisions cooked before hand and keep them together as much as possible night and day that they may be in readiness in the shortest notice to make head against the enemy."

Before the day of the twelfth was over a letter from Colonel Joseph Reed was handed to General Washington, just to make certain that he would sleep poorly if at all. The letter from Joseph Reed read as follows:

"Dear Sir—The gentlemen of the Light Horse who went into the Jerseys have returned safe. They preceded into the country till they met an intelligent person directly from Trenton, who informed them that General Howe was then with the main body of his army: that the flying army, consisting of the Light Infantry and Grenadiers, under Lord Cornwallis, still lay at Pennytown and there was no appearance of a movement, that they are certainly waiting for boats from Brunswick; that he believed they would attempt a landing in more places than one; that their artillery park has thirty pieces of cannon—all field pieces. They are collecting horses from all parts of the country. Some movement was intended yesterday morning but laid aside; but what it was and why they did not proceed he does not know. I sent off a person to Trenton yesterday morning with directions to return by Pennytown. I told him to go to——and to get what intelligence he could from him. He has not yet returned. I expect him every moment. I charged him to let——know that, if he would watch their motions and the performance of the time and place of their proposed landing, he should receive a large reward for which I would be answerable. I cannot but think but that their landing will be between this and Trenton. . . ."

NOTES: Chapter 19

Charles M. Lefferts, in his astonishing (and often inventive) book on uniforms of the Revolution, shows the Jägers with cocked hats and leggings instead of boots. They were unquestionably the best and most practical soldiers of their time, and they were the only British-commanded regiment to use both rifle and bayonet. The capture of some of the Jägers at Trenton is the highest tribute to what the Americans accomplished.

What follows is Lefferts' description of the Field Jäger Corps of Hesse-Cassel:

"This rifle corps had detachments in almost every skirmish and battle of the American Revolution. The Brunswick and Anspach yagers or chasseurs wore the same dress but with bright red facings and linings to the coats. On parade, they wore tall green feathers in their hats above the green silk cockade, and in summer white linen breeches. Officers were distinguished by a white feather, and gold lace on the cuffs and lapels. Sergeants by a white feather with red top, and gold lace on the cuffs. Their whole uniform was much superior to those of the line regiments, and they were considered a 'Corps d'élite.' "

NOTES: Chapter 22

Most of the detailed information concerning the capture of General Charles Lee at Baskingridge by the British derives from the journal of James Wilkinson. This fascinating book was titled *Memoirs of My Own Times*, and was published in Philadelphia in 1816. However, there were some other points of view.

Joseph Trumbull, commissary general of the army, wrote to Governor Trumbull soon after Lee's capture, setting down the story of the Tory and the stolen horse, and confirmation of this incident came from British sources. Fonblanque, in his *Life of General Burgoyne*, mentions that the Queen's Light Dragoons—who effected the capture—were a part of Burgoyne's command and had acted much as Wilkinson states. The dragoons, in this case, were under the command of Cornet Banastre Tarleton. Major William Bradford of Rhode Island specifies the Tory as one James Compton, who lived in Baskingridge. Tarleton stated afterward that his troopers had surrounded the inn when they effected Lee's capture. So the escape of Major Wilkinson remains a mystery.

The following documents relate the capture of General Lee.

Banastre Tarleton to his mother.

Prince's Town, December 18, 1776

My dear Madam

Our correspondence is totally stopt, so few ships go to and come from England on acct. of the quantity of American privateers that this continent seems utterly secluded from Great Britain.

You will with pleasure, if you receive it, read this letter. Lieutenant General Earl Cornwallis, under whose command the King's army has penetrated into the Jerseys as far as the River Delaware, being ignorant of General Lee's motions and situation, gave orders on the 11th inst. for a party of the Queen's Light Dragoons, consisting of a captain, 2 subalterns and 25 privates, to be ready to march in expedition order the next morning. Colonel Harcourt who was with the regiment received his private orders from Lord Cornwallis, together with Captain Eustace, his Lordship's aid de camp, who attended us on this expedition.

Our first day's march was 18 miles, but barren of incidents. We took up our quarters at night at Hillsborough upon the River Millstone. A battalion of the 71st covered us at that place. Our house caught fire at 1 o'clock in the morning and burnt to the ground. We escaped without loss or damage—we bedded ourselves in straw till 5 o'clock. We then received orders to march. Col. Harcourt gave me the advanced guard, consisting of 6 men: a circumstance I ever shall esteem as one of the most fortunate of my life. We marched by different and cross roads towards Maurice Town. We had not proceeded above 14 miles before the advanced guard discovered some and took one Rebel in arms. We marched 2 miles forward, then Colonel Harcourt found by some people that General Lee was not above 4 or 5 miles distant from the detachment, and at the same time heard that our retreat was cut off by the road we had come. He detached Captain Nash with 4 dragoons back to prove the truth of the last information. Colonel Harcourt then ordered me to advance. We trotted on about 3 miles when my advanced guard seized 2 sentrys without firing a gun.

The dread of instant death obliged these fellows to inform me, to the best of my knowledge, of the situation of General Lee. They told us he was about a mile off, that his guard was not very large and that he was about half a mile in the rear of his army. These men were so confused that they gave us but an imperfect idea where General Lee was. Colonel Harcourt immediately detached me with 2 men only to the top of an eminence in the road, to get what intelligence I could, and if much fired upon, immediately to retreat upon him. In going quick to the ground I observed a Yankee light-horseman, at whom I rushed and made prisoner. I brought him in to Colonel Harcourt; the fear of the sabre extorted great intelligence, and he told us he had just left General Lee from whom he had an express to carry to General Sullivan at Pukamin [*sic*]. He could not satisfy me exactly as to the strength of General Lee's guard, but confirmed the account of the other 2 prisoners as to his situation.

He said he thought his guard did not consist of above 30 men. He pointed out to us the house where he had left General Lee and mentioned that he was going to move directly.

Colonel Harcourt called to Eustace, to know whether he thought we were strong enough. Eustace replyed in the affirmative. Without further consultation I was ordered to lead on my advanced guard which consisted of only 5 men as quick as possible. I went on at full speed, when perceiving two sentrys at a door and a loaded waggon I pushed at them, making all the noise I could. The sentrys were struck with a panic, dropped their arms and fled. I ordered my men to fire into the house thro' every window and door, and cut up as many of the guard as they could. An old woman upon her knees begged for life and told me General Lee was in the house.

This assurance gave me pleasure. I carried on my attack with all possible spirit and surrounded the house, tho' fired upon in front, flank and rear. General Lee's aid de camp, 2 French colonels and some of the guard kept up a fire for about 8 minutes, which we silenced. I fired twice through the door of the house and then addressed myself to this effect: "I knew Genl. Lee was in the house, that if he would surrender himself, he and his attendants should be safe, but if my summons was not complied with immediately, the house should be burnt and every person without exception should be put to the sword."

At this instant I was called by one of my men to the back door, my attention being directly engaged by his saying that Genl. Lee was escaping that way and I galloped to the spot. The French colonels, one of the aid de camp (the other being shot) and some of the guard attempted to retreat sword in hand. We took one colonel prisoner, the rest were killed or wounded. Genl. Lee surrendered himself to the sentry I had placed at the front door, whilst we were employed as above. The prisoner was led to Col. Harcourt, who was silencing the fires in my rear and flanks whilst I carried on the attack upon Genl. Lee's quarters with the advanced guard only. Col. Harcourt placed his noble prisoner upon a horse and led him off by a different road from that which we had come with all possible expedition.

The bugle horn was then sounded. I brought up the rear of the men and the French colonel. This attack which continued in the whole about 15 minutes proved fatal to none of the officers or dragoons. One horse's leg which was slightly grazed and one saddle which was shot through the pommel were the only damages we sustained. We retreated afterwards 13 miles thro' an enemys country without any accident. We then forded a river, approached Hillsborough and gave each other congratulations with every symptom of joy.

Captain Nash whom I mentioned being detached did not join us again till Genl. Lee was our prisoner. He was beat back from the place where we had passed in the morning and where they meant to cut off our retreat. He lost a servant and a horse. The party returned safe.

This is a most miraculous event—it appears like a dream. We conducted Genl. Lee and the French col. to Lord Cornwallis at Penning. Our day's march only exceeded 60 miles.

Genl. Lee is sent prisoner to Brunswick. Colonel Harcourt's whole conduct was masterly—it deserves every applause. Present my love, comps., etc. (I shall tire you if I write any more).

I forgot to tell you that this coup de main has put an end to the campaign. We have not yet crossed the Delaware. The Queen's Regt. of Lt. Dragoons are cantoned off Princes Town and Brunswick; at the former exists one who will always be proud to subscribe himself

Your affectionate son

BANASTRE TARLETON

—BASS, *The Green Dragoon*, pp. 20–22.

Memoirs of Captain James Wilkinson of the Continental Army.

General Lee wasted the morning in altercation with certain militia corps who were of his command, particularly the Connecticut light horse, several of whom appeared in large full-bottomed perukes, and were treated very irreverently; the call of the adjutant general for orders also occupied some of his time, and we did not sit down to breakfast before 10 o'clock. General Lee was engaged in answering General Gates's letter, and I had risen from the table and was looking out of an end window down a lane about one hundred yards in length which led to the house from the main road, when I discovered a party of British dragoons turn a corner of the avenue at a full charge.

Startled at this unexpected spectacle, I exclaimed, "Here, Sir, are the British cavalry!"

"Where?" replied the general, who had signed his letter in the instant.

"Around the house;" for they had opened files and encompassed the building.

General Lee appeared alarmed, yet collected, and his second observation marked his self-possession: "Where is the guard?—damn the guard, why don't they fire?" and after a momentary pause, he turned to me and said, "Do, Sir, see what has become of the guard."

The women of the house at this moment entered the room and proposed to him to conceal himself in a bed, which he rejected with evident disgust. I caught up my pistols which lay on the table, thrust the letter he had been writing into my pocket, and passed into a room at the opposite end of the house, where I had seen the guard in the morning. Here I discovered their arms; but the men were absent. I stepped out of the door and perceived the dragoons chasing them in different directions, and receiving a very uncivil salutation, I returned into the house.

Too inexperienced immediately to penetrate the motives of this enterprize, I considered the *rencontre* accidental, and from the terrific tales spread over the country of the violence and barbarity of the enemy, I believed it to be a wanton murdering party, and determined not to die without company. I accordingly sought a position where I could not be approached by more than one person at a time, and with a pistol in each hand I awaited the expected search, resolved to shoot the first and the second person who might appear, and then to appeal to my sword. I did not remain long in this unpleasant situation, but was apprised of the object of the incursion by the very audible declaration, *"If the general does not surrender in five minutes, I will set fire to the house;"* which after a short pause was repeated with a solemn oath; and within two minutes I heard it proclaimed, *"Here is the general. He has surrendered."* A general shout ensued, the trumpet sounded the assembly, and the unfortunate Lee mounted on my horse, which stood ready at the door, was hurried off in triumph, bareheaded, in his slippers and blanket coat, his collar open, and his shirt very much soiled from several days' use.

—WILKINSON, *Memoirs of My Own Times*, 1, 105–106.

Who to believe—Wilkinson or Tarleton? Both liars, both scoundrels, both men of small honor. History is filled with such alternate versions of the "truth." Lee was captured—that is all we truly know. As for the "two French Colonels," they remain one of the curious enigmas of the history of the Revolution.

NOTES FOR *The Second Crossing*
(WEST *to* EAST)

NOTES: *Chapter* 4

It is perhaps too easy to use General Horatio Gates as a villain. History has structured him as the prime internal enemy of General Washington, and the so-called Conway Cabal was taught to generations of young Americans as proof of Gates's infamy. But the infamy was more of a scholarly creation than a fact of the time, and his rivalry with Washington becomes far more understandable if one sees it as the rivalry of the agrarian democrat with the aristocrat—for all that Gates was British-born.

In John C. Miller's *Triumph of Freedom*, Little, Brown and Company, 1948, there is an excellent description of the Gates—Washington feud (pp. 234–261), one that upsets certain notions of Continental unity behind Washington. Thoughtful and respected men like Dr. Benjamin Rush and James Lovell honored Gates and despised Washington, while others, Thomas Paine, Nathanael Greene, Henry Knox to mention only a few, worshiped the ground Washington walked upon. Paine's adoration of Washington was not unconnected with his later miseries, and Lord Stirling, so close to Washington, was denounced as a fool and a drunkard by Washington's enemies.

It appeared to me—with some logic, I believe—that the Gates—Washington split began actively just before the crossing, with

Gates's cold rejection of Washington's daring scheme. Upon this, I reconstructed the content of a meeting of which we have no exact record.

The separation between these two men was very deep and many-sided, even extending to Mrs. Gates's jealousy of Martha Washington and her bitterness at the public adulation offered to Martha. Gates believed in short-term militia; Washington believed in a trained, professional army. The differences went on, too numerous to specify here.

NOTES: *Chapter* 14

When the meeting at the Merrick house finally wound up, Washington dictated the following order:

Each brigade to be furnished with two good guides. General Stephen's brigade to form the advance party, and to have with them a detachment of the artillery without cannon, provided with spikes and hammers to spike up the enemy's cannon in case of necessity, or to bring them off if it can be effected, the party to be provided with drag-ropes for the purpose of dragging cannon. General Stephen is to attack and force the enemy's guards and seize such posts as may prevent them from forming in the streets, and in case they are annoyed from the houses to set them on fire. The brigades of Mercer and Lord Stirling, under the command of Major General Green, support General Stephen. This is the second division or left wing of the army and to march by the way of the Pennington road.

St. Clair's, Glover's and Sargent's brigades under Major General Sullivan, to march by the River road. This is the first division of the army, and to form the right wing. Lord Stirling's brigade to form the reserve of the left wing, and General St. Clair's brigade the reserve of the right wing. These reserves to form a second line in conjunction, or a second line to each division, as circumstances may require. Each Brigadier to make the Colonels acquainted with the posts of their respective regiments in the brigade, and the Major Generals will inform them of the posts of the brigades in the line. Four pieces of artillery to march at the head of each column; three pieces at the head of the second brigade of each division; and two pieces with each of the reserves. The troops to be assembled one mile back of McKonkey's Ferry, and as soon as it begins to grow dark the troops to be marched to McKonkey's Ferry, and embark on board the boats in the following order under the direction of Colonel Knox.

General Stephen's brigade, with the detachment of artillery men, to embark first; General Mercer's next; Lord Stirling's next; General Fermoy's next, who will march into the rear of the second division and file off from the Pennington to the Princeton road in such direction that he can with the greatest ease and safety secure the passes between Princeton and Trenton. The guides will be the best judges of this. He is to take two pieces of artillery with him. St. Clair's, Glover's, and Sargent's brigades to embark in order. Immediately upon their debarkation, the whole to form and march in subdivisions from the right. The commanding officers of regiments to observe that the divisions be equal and that proper officers be appointed to each. A profound silence to be enjoined, and no man to quit his ranks on the pain of death. Each Brigadier to appoint flanking parties; the reserve brigades to appoint the rear guards of the columns; the heads of the columns to be appointed to arrive at Trenton at five o'clock.

Captain Washington and Captain Flahaven, with a party of forty men each, to march before the divisions and post themselves on the road about three miles from Trenton, and make prisoners of all going in or going out of the town.

General Stephen will appoint a guard to form a chain of sentries round the landing place at a sufficient distance from the river to permit the troops to form, this guard not to suffer any person to go in or come out, but to detain all persons who attempt either. This guard to join their brigade when the troops are all over.

* * *

Such was the general order drawn up at the meeting by General Washington and with the advice of his staff officers. Stryker, in his book on the Battle of Trenton, quotes one of the several orders drawn up for the brigade leaders to send to their colonels as a specific of instruction for the crossing, and we have the text of this example that General Mercer sent to Colonel Durkee later the same evening or possibly after midnight, since the meeting went on into the small hours of the morning:

"Sir: You are to see that your men have three days provisions ready cooked before 12 o'clock this forenoon—the whole fit for duty except a Sergeant and six men to be left with the baggage, and to parade precisely at four in the afternoon with their arms, accoutrements and ammunition in the best order, with their provisions and blankets—you will have then told off in divisions in which order they are to march—eight men abreast, with the officers fixed to their divisions from which they are on no account to separate—no man is to quit his division on pain of instant punishment—each officer is to provide himself with a piece of white paper stuck in his hat for a field mark. You will order your men to assemble and parade them in the valley immediately over the hill on the back of McConkey's Ferry, to remain there for further orders—a profound silence is to be observed, both by officers and men, and a strict and ready attention paid to whatever orders may be given—in forming the Brigade Co. Durkee takes the right, Co. Stone left, Co. Bradley on the left of Co. Durkee and Co. Rawlings on the right of Co. Stone—the Line to form and march from the Right—Co. Hutchinson to form by themselves."

We note that *McKonkey*, as with so many names in field orders, is spelled in various fashions. The name of Rahl, the Hessian commander, was also spelled Rall and Ruhl.

NOTES: *Chapter* 19

What follows is an extract from a memorandum in General Robert Anderson's letter book. This extract purports to solve the mystery of who fired at the Hessians at five o'clock on the twenty-fifth of December 1776. To my thinking it does not; however, it must be admitted as a historical curiosity. Speaking of his father, Captain Richard Clough Anderson of the 5th Regiment of the Continental Infantry, Robert Anderson wrote:

His orders were to reconnoitre, to see where the enemy's outpost were, to get such information as he could about them, but to be very careful and not to bring on an engagement.

Having gone to the places designated without finding the enemy, he advanced upon Trenton. The party came close upon the Hessian sentinal, who was marching on his post, bending his head down as he met the storm, which beat heavily in the driving snow in the faces of the patrol. He saw them about the same time that he was seen, and as he brought his gun to a charge and challenged, he was shot down. My father having now accomplished the object of his mission, and knowing the enemy's forces would be promptly turned out, and that an engagement which he had been ordered to avoid would ensue, ordered his company to countermarch, and marched them back towards his camp. He had not gone far before he saw, very much to his surprise, Washington's army advancing toward him. As he was there in a narrow lane he ordered his company to withdraw one side into an adjoining field. The advance guard seeing the body of soldiers ahead, and supposing they were the advance guard of the British forces, halted, and very soon an officer approached near enough to recognize them as American troops. General Washington approached and asked him who was in command and where he had been. I have frequently heard my father remark that he never saw Genl. Washington exhibit so much anger as he did when he told him where he had been and what he had done. He turned to Genl. Stephen and asked how he dared to send a patrol from camp without his authority, remarking, you sir may have ruined all my plans, by having put them on their guard. He then addressed my father in a very calm and considerate manner and told him that as he and his men must be very much fatigued after such hard service, he should march in the vanguard, where he would be less harassed by the fatigue of the march.

This curious memorandum is quoted by William Stryker, but it does not to my satisfaction answer the problem of who attacked the Hessian camp at 5 P.M. on Christmas Day. For one thing, this account speaks of only a single shot and only of the sentry being killed. There was quite a volley of shots, and three Hessians were killed and three more were wounded. What may be the truth of the circumstances surrounding this memorandum of Robert Anderson's will possibly never be known.

NOTES: *Chapter* 20

We do not know whether Washington's angry letter reached Cadwalader that night. We do know that the two other divisions of his army were already accepting defeat. General Ewing with his fifteen hundred men never really made a serious attempt to cross. His men were reluctant, and he hadn't the guts to force the issue. He finally bowed to the ferocity of the weather and the ice in the river. This crossing, a mile to the south of Trenton, would have supported Washington and opened the attack upon Trenton from the south.

As to what occurred at Bristol, where Colonel Cadwalader, now brevetted General Cadwalader, was in command, we have a very clear and definite account in a letter by Thomas Rodney to Caesar Rodney, which he wrote on December 30, 1776:

On the 25th inst. in the evening, we received orders to be at Shamony Ferry as soon as possible. We were there according to orders in two hours, and met the riflemen, who were the first from Bristol; we were ordered from thence to Dunk's Ferry, on the Delaware, and the whole army of about 2,000 men followed as soon as the artillery got up. The three companies, a Philadelphia infantry and mine were formed into a body, under the command of Captain Henry (myself second in command), which were embarked immediately to cover the landing of the other troops.

We landed with great difficulty through the ice, and formed on the farther shore, about 200 yards from the river. It was as severe a night as ever I saw, and after two battalions were landed, the storm increased so much and the river was so full of ice, that it was impossible to get the artillery over; for we had to walk 100 yards on the ice to get on shore. General Cadwalader therefore ordered the whole to retreat again, and we had to stand at least six hours under arms—first to cover the landing until all the rest had retreated again—and, by this time, the storm of wind, hail, rain and snow, with the ice, was so bad that some of the infantry could not get back till next day. This design was to have surprised the enemy at Black Horse and Mount Holley, at the same time that Washington surprised them at Trenton; and had we succeeded in getting over, we should have finished all our troubles.

NOTES: *Chapter* 22

Concerning the wet flints and powder during the night march in the rain, when Sullivan sent Captain Mott to Washington for instructions, our best information comes from Washington Irving's *Life of George Washington.* According to Irving, Washington's reply to Mott's demand as to what they should do without guns that would not fire was an "indignant burst," but anyone knowing of Washington's gift for words in such moments of stress must conclude that his reply was more than an "indignant burst." Again according to Washington Irving, he told the runner to return and tell Sullivan to "advance and charge!" But it is within the framework of probability to conclude that Washington's instructions were more emphatic and more colorful than anything Irving could put to paper at the time he wrote.

NOTES: *Chapter* 30

The Hessian losses are confirmed in a map that was drawn on the fifteenth of April, 1777, by William Faden, a British cartographer, who sold the map at St. Martin's Lane, Charing Cross, London. The map shows the details of the crossing, the march on Trenton and the battle. It also enumerates Hessian losses in both men and munitions.

We also have available the proceedings of the courts-martial of the Hessian officers—selections translated by Washington Irving (*Life of George Washington*) and by William S. Stryker, *The Battles of Trenton and Princeton.*

The most interesting details of this strange battle can be found in the Hessian accounts.